KILLER KOOL

A Mango Bay Mystery

Other Books by Marty Ambrose

The Mango Bay Mystery Series:
Peril in Paradise
Island Intrigue
Murder in the Mangroves

KILLER KOOL

•

Marty Ambrose

AVALON BOOKS
NEW YORK

© Copyright 2011 by Marty Ambrose
All rights reserved.
All the characters in this book are fictitious,
and any resemblance to actual persons,
living or dead, is purely coincidental.
Published by Avalon Books,
an imprint of Thomas Bouregy & Co., Inc.
160 Madison Avenue, New York, NY 10016

Library of Congress Cataloging-in-Publication Data

Ambrose, Marty.
    Killer Kool : a Mango Bay mystery / Marty Ambrose.
        p. cm.
    ISBN 978-0-8034-7608-0 (hardcover : alk. paper)
    1. Women journalists—Fiction.   2. Murder—
Investigation—Fiction.   3. Florida—Fiction.   I. Title.
    PS3601.M368K55 2011
    813'.6—dc22
                                              2011018713

PRINTED IN THE UNITED STATES OF AMERICA
ON ACID-FREE PAPER
BY RR DONNELLEY, BLOOMSBURG, PENNSYLVANIA

Acknowledgments

I would to thank my Mom, the real "Delores," for all her help and support during my writing career. She is simply the best mother one could ever wish for. Many thanks to my husband and sister for always being there with editorial advice as well.

My sincere gratitude to my editor, Lia Brown, whose suggestions improve my books on every level.

Last, but not least, are my heartfelt thanks to my agent and friend, Roberta Brown. My writing career is largely due to her positive support of me as a writer.

"I want my food dead. Not sick, not dying, dead."
—Oscar Wilde

Chapter One

We need to shake things up—now!" my editor, Anita Sanders, pronounced as she breezed into our newspaper office. "It's almost Halloween, and we're still doing stories about hurricane season preparedness. Boring!"

"You mean you don't like this article on 'The ABCs of Disaster Supply Kits'?" I pointed at my computer screen. Okay, so it was a big yawn. Our little southwest Florida island had officially hit the early-fall doldrums—and so had the front-page stories on our Coral Island weekly paper, the *Observer*. Not that I wanted a hurricane to hit—far from it. But Anita had a point: we needed something fresh, new, and exciting to jazz up our headlines. And to keep me from falling asleep at the keyboard.

"Spare me. All I need after a hurricane is a jar of peanut butter and a bottle of bourbon." Her mouth twisted upward in a slight smile, deepening the lines in her thin face. Hard-edged, fiftyish, and a former reporter for the *Detroit Free Press*, Anita had little patience with people who lived cautiously—or who didn't ravage their appearance with cigarettes and booze. She'd popped out of the womb as a three-pack-a-day smoker, having stopped only recently. But the damage was done.

"Let's see . . . how about my interview with Harry "the Hurricane Boy" Torino, who was selling boxed emergency kits at the island center?" I offered, swiveling my new chair in her direction. Now that Anita was dating Mr. Benton, the old cheapskate had finally funneled a little money into the office—stress the word *little*: some paint, an indoor-outdoor carpet in pea green, and secondhand, instead of thirdhand, furniture. At least I didn't have to worry that the rollers might fall off my chair every time I leaned backward. And my refurbished Dell computer was only three years old, not ten.

"Pffffft. Harry is a scam artist. All those kits have in them is dried fruit, SPAM, and waterless shampoo. That's going to be a *big* help after a hurricane." She sat on the corner of my desk and pulled out a tube of lipstick from her purse. *Lipstick?!* She coated her mouth with a bright orange swipe of color. *Yikes.* Then I scanned her face more closely and realized that she was also wearing foundation and mascara. Of course, the makeup had settled in her smoker's wrinkles, and the mascara had smudged under her eyes, giving her a raccoonlike look. *Double yikes.*

"Anita, are you wearing . . . uh . . . cosmetics?" I said in disbelief.

"Yup." She pulled out a compact and swept the puff across her cheeks in a thick line. "I went into town and had a makeover. Bought myself the basics. I gotta keep up now that I have a boyfriend."

I swallowed hard. Mr. Benton was close to seventy and looked like Mr. Potato Head with a bad toupee. But, hey, if having a man made Anita a little nicer, I'd buy them a gift certificate for dinner at the Starfish Lodge—Coral Island's nicest restaurant (translated: you had to wear shoes).

"And I'm not stopping with the makeover. I'm going to the next level: the heavy-duty stuff," Anita continued as she slapped a brochure onto my desk. "The island dermatologist is now offering full-service rejuvenation."

I glanced down at the tri-fold paper brochure with the caption: *Beauty Is in the Eye of the Bee Holder!* Underneath were "Before and After" pictures of a woman who looked eighty, and then twenty, courtesy of a miracle bee cream, some kind of injectable gook, and (in my opinion) major heavy-handed Photoshopping.

Uh-oh.

"I'm starting with the bee cream tonight. The main ingredient is one hundred percent pure, island-grown bee pollen—right from the hives." She held up a small jar and opened the lid.

I sniffed and then gagged. It smelled like an old shoe. Anita scooped out a lump and dabbed a small amount on the crow's-feet next to her eyes, careful not to smear her makeup. Then she rubbed the rest on her neck. "It's supposed to smooth out all the lines in a week."

A sandblaster might help more, but I kept that thought to myself.

"Okay, enough about my getting gorgeous." She replaced the lid and tossed the cream and lipstick into her purse. "Let's talk about spicing up our October stories enough so I don't have to prop my eyes open with sticks to read them."

I clicked on my computer calendar that listed all of the upcoming island events. "We've got the Halloween face-painting contest at the elementary school."

"Yawn."

"How about the Fall Fish Toss?"

"Asleep."

I sighed. "I guess we're down to the Autumn Book Fair."

"Comatose."

I leaned back in my chair and folded my arms across my chest, sighing. Coral Island was a twenty-mile-long strip of land that ran north–south inside of the coastal barrier islands, which meant only a tiny beach, few tourists, and even fewer happenings that didn't involve kids, fishing, and Rotary Clubs. "I'm out of events . . . except this food thing coming up—"

"Jeez, how could I have forgotten?" She rapped herself on the forehead. "It's the first annual 'Taste of the Island' next weekend. Perfect!"

"Great." I managed a weak smile, but even I could hear the lack of enthusiasm in my voice. I wasn't a big foodie, to say the least. Mostly, I survived on coffee, Krispy Kreme doughnuts, fast food, and the occasional chocolate energy bars when I thought I needed something healthy.

"Listen, kiddo, this is a biggie. Every restaurant on Coral Island will have a booth, and people can sample their trademark food all day. Then they'll vote on the best restaurant. Benton filled me in, since he's in the island Chamber of Commerce that planned it—a real family event."

"And you *liked* the idea?" I could feel my eyes widen. Anita hated wholesome, even more than she disliked dull.

"Hell, no." She stood up. "But I *love* the idea of all the island restaurants competing for the honor of winning Best Sauce, Best Appetizer, or Best Dog Chow at the event. I'm sure they'll do anything to win: steal recipes, spy on one another's waitstaff, find ways to spike a competing chef's food with ingredients that make people sick. Oh, yes, I *love* it." She rubbed her hands together with glee.

Only Anita would be excited at the thought of people with food poisoning. "I guess I can interview a few of the restaurant owners this week—"

"No. No. No." She shook her head each time she repeated the word. "You're going to visit each restaurant and sample the food; then you can write about it. You'll have a blog this week as the new food critic for the *Observer,* and then do updates twice a day."

I gasped. The Coral Island restaurants weren't exactly Maxim's. My least favorite, Le Sink, served (from what I'd heard) only charred hamburgers in its open-air serving space and had ceramic sinks littered all around the yard.

"Let's start with Le Sink."

Of course. "But, Anita—"

"No *buts.*" She held up a hand. "This is just what we need to spice things up, literally." Cackling at her own pun, she strolled into her tiny office, as she smoothed another layer of the bee cream onto her arms.

Just then Sandy, our receptionist-cum-secretary-cum-anything, strolled in carrying a stack of wedding magazines. She halted and sniffed. "What's that weird smell?"

"Bee face cream." I tilted my head in the direction of Anita's office. "She's on some kind of weird beauty kick to keep Mr. Benton 'forever panting, and forever young.'"

I couldn't resist the Keats quotation. I'd majored in comparative literature—a degree that opened the doors of the underemployed at every junction of my journey from the Midwest to Florida. But at least I could always come up with a catchy quote.

Sandy picked up the brochure and nodded sagely. "Love will do that to you. I know I always want to look my best for Jimmy." A soft glow lit her sweetly featured face. "You would think it was spring instead of fall with all the love in the air." She grinned, tucking a strand of nut-brown hair behind her ear.

I couldn't help smiling back. Sandy had gotten engaged over the last summer to Jimmy, the son of our freelance island psychic, Madame Geri, and her life had turned golden. Sandy had found the man of her dreams, lost twenty pounds, ditched the Coke-bottle glasses for contacts, and started making extra money writing obituaries for the newspaper. If I didn't know better, I would swear Madame Geri had put a happy spell on Sandy.

"What about you?" Sandy asked as she set the magazines on her desk that faced mine. "Isn't it great having your boyfriend back?"

I paused. My ex-boyfriend, Cole Whitney, had made a summer appearance at the Twin Palms RV Resort where I had parked my Airstream trailer and teacup poodle, King Kong, two years ago. I'd missed Cole terribly right after he had taken off from our place in Orlando to "find himself" out west, but after all my adventures on Coral Island, someone new had appeared on the horizon— Nick Billie, the local island cop.

"I like having Cole around again, but, well, it's just different." I shrugged.

"Now that Detective Billie is in the running," she added with a knowing grin.

"That's not true exactly. And it's not a race. More like a crawl." Sighing, I leaned my head in my hands. This whole relationship thing between old boyfriend and possible new boyfriend seemed like getting stuck in a sand hole on the beach. I couldn't see it coming, and I didn't know how to get out—or even if I wanted to. "I can't be bothered with figuring out men. Cole is like a butterfly, and Nick is like a granite bust—both just as frustrating. I think I'm going to stick with Kong. It's a lot easier."

"So you say." She seated herself at her desk. "Just remember: it's no fun snuggling up to a dog on a hot, tropical night."

True.

"Some women would think you're in the catbird seat: torn between two handsome men," Sandy continued as she turned on her computer. "Not me, of course. Jimmy is all I need in my life."

"He's a gem." I wasn't lying or even stretching the truth. Stocky, good-humored, and hardworking, Jimmy really *was* a gem.

"Thanks, Mallie." She picked up the brochure about the bee cream and scanned it. "You know, I might try some of this stuff. I want my skin to look perfect on my wedding day."

"But it's only two weeks away. I'm not sure what kind of results you can get that fast," I pointed out, eyeing those phony before-and-after pictures again. "Worst case scenario, your skin might turn yellow."

"Or I might grow wings." She laughed.

"Just so you don't fly away. Jimmy would be devastated." I snatched the brochure back. "The only thing Anita seems to have grown is a stinger—right in her—"

"Okay, I've got the picture. But she had that before she tried the face cream." Sandy laughed, waiting for her ancient computer to fire up. Mr. Benton hadn't updated all of the technology in our little newspaper office, but maybe that was next, especially if Anita turned into some kind of middle-aged siren for stingy bosses.

Fat chance.

"Maybe *you* should buy some of the cream; it might

help, since you're always complaining about your freckles," Sandy said, eyeing my pale, freckled skin.

"I've changed my opinion over the last year that I've lived in Florida. I now prefer to call them beauty spots." I fluffed my wild profusion of scarlet curls that accompanied the typical redhead's skin. "I read somewhere that skin without freckles is like a sky without stars." Hey, it sounded good, and what was the use in fighting my skin under the tropical sun? Besides, I'd already tried freckle removal cream, freckle fade cream, and freckle laser removal. (Okay, I'd only *thought* about the last one—I didn't have the money to give it a try.) None of them worked. In fact, I now had *more* freckles.

"Just as well," Sandy said. "I like 'em. They suit you." She tapped on her keyboard and then fastened her glance on the screen. "What's on your calendar this week?"

"Hold your breath—my main story isn't logged in yet." I paused for effect. "I'm the *Observer*'s new food critic for the upcoming 'Taste of the Island.'"

"Oh, wow. What I wouldn't give for that assignment. I'm so sick of writing obits." She glanced down at her midsized thighs with a sigh and gave them a little pat. "But with only two weeks before my wedding, I couldn't be a food anything—I'd never fit into my dress."

"Before you get too nostalgic for your triple-chocolate ice cream days, you might want to know where I'm having lunch."

"The Starfish Lodge?"

I shook my head at the name of the island's best restaurant.

Don't I wish.

"The Seafood Shanty?"

"Nope." Their specialty—warm beer and peanuts—
sounded good.

She held up her palms in baffled anticipation.

"Le Sink."

"No!" Sandy gasped and swallowed audibly. "I thought
the Board of Health closed down their kitchen."

"I guess they opened up again."

"You'd better lay in a stock of Pepto-Bismol. I've
heard the hamburgers are . . . well, hard to digest." She
grimaced.

"You're being diplomatic," I said. "I've heard the food
can burn a hole in your stomach as wide as the Gulf of
Mexico. Kind of gives a whole new meaning to 'junk
food.' And that's pretty strong talk coming from someone like me who eats three doughnuts for breakfast with
a half gallon of coffee for a chaser."

"Well, maybe you could just take a nibble and then
write the review," she offered with an encouraging nod.
"That might not be too bad."

"I think I'll have to eat more than just one bite to
write a review." I groaned, closing my eyes for a brief
moment. "Why is it Anita always comes up with an assignment that seems more like a prison sentence?" I'd
been working at the *Observer* for over a year, and I still
covered mostly senior-center events and cutesy-kid sto-

ries. No matter what I did, it was never good enough for her. Just like my mother.

Oh, jeez. Where had that come from? Was that why I stayed? To prove myself?

Okay, too heavy. I made a practice of no self-analysis before lunch—or after. I liked to take life just as it comes—at face value.

"She can't help it, Mallie. Remember what Madame Geri said about Anita? She's a Gemini and likes to do things her own way, even when it seems like a whim to everyone else. You have to ride out her craziness." Sandy gave a knowing wink. "Now that she's dating Mr. Benton, maybe he'll rein her in a bit."

"Since when did you get so wise?"

"Hey, I'm marrying Madame Geri's son—I've got a pipeline to the psychic truth." She tilted her head upward as if her prospective mother-in-law were some kind of divine presence. "I feel almost like I'm marrying into royalty."

More like a noble nutcase.

"I know you don't always agree with Madame Geri," Sandy continued, focusing on me again. "But you have to admit, at times she's really awesome."

I restrained myself from rolling my eyes. Madame Geri, though worshipped on the island like some kind of tropical Oracle of Delphi, made predictions one step up from a fortune cookie. Still, she occasionally hit the mark—and that scared me. One of my many jobs had been at a psychic hotline, and I was a total sham. Just listening and responding with "uh-huh" and "oh, no" was the extent of my mystic abilities. Most of the people who called knew what they wanted to do; they just needed a willing ear at $1.99 a minute.

But one woman who'd worked with me, Irene, had stunned me with her "reads" over the phone. She *always* knew the truth behind every caller's dilemma—totally intimidating.

In fact, I'd been tempted to call her many times after I'd left yet another job, but I didn't want to know my future.

That scared me even more.

Sandy glanced at me, still waiting for a response.

"Yeah, Madame Geri is a . . . piece of work all right," I managed to get out.

Sandy shook her head. "You'll agree someday. She's generally right on target."

"I hardly need a prediction to know how my first dining experience as the *Observer* food critic is going to turn out." I turned on my computer and Googled *Le Sink*, while Sandy clicked away on an obituary. Surprisingly, they had a Web site with a picture of the actual restaurant (and I use that term loosely). It appeared to consist of an open-air counter with "picnic table seating" and variously colored old ceramic sinks littered around the yard. "Do you think they clean these tables?" I turned my computer screen toward Sandy.

"Rarely," she answered without a glance. "I went there

once with Jimmy. We had to wait two hours for our dinner, and it was . . . Well, you'll see."

I groaned again.

"Oh, and don't use the Porta Potti. It's beyond nasty. You could slap a saddle onto the palmetto bugs and ride them out of there."

"You're not helping much."

"I'm just trying to be honest. Forewarned is forearmed," Sandy murmured as she kept clicking on her keyboard. It always amazed me when she could simultaneously hang on the phone, type on her computer, and carry on a conversation without a blink—or losing her train of thought. Sandy's uber-ability to multitask was legendary on Coral Island, which is why Anita kept her employed at the *Observer*, even during her borderline "price tag" years, when Sandy wouldn't cut the tags off her clothes because her weight kept fluctuating. Anita feared the newspaper might lose potential clothing store advertisers.

Of course, Anita would've fired *me* for jaywalking in the office.

"Whose obit are you working on?" I asked, not able to look any longer at the grimy scene that awaited me at Le Sink.

"Carlos Santini. His brother owns one of the better restaurants on the island, Little Tuscany. It's a nice place—unlike Le Sink. Great food, nice atmosphere, and no fried food . . ."

"Oops, you had me until the last one. I never said I didn't like grease." Okay, so I wasn't exactly top shelf when it came to dining out. But Nick Billie hadn't done much more than buy me a grouper sandwich at the Seafood Shanty, and Cole rarely had enough cash to do more than grill out at the RV park.

Maybe I needed a better-quality guy in my life. I had two of them, but neither one treated me to *haute cuisine* or "haughty cruising," as Wanda Sue, my landlady at the Twin Palms RV Resort, pronounced it.

"What happened to Carlos Santini?" I asked.

"Don't know. He had angina, so they think he probably had a heart attack, but he was only in his midfifties. I guess the police wanted an autopsy because he died at home."

I took a peek at the photo on Sandy's screen. Dark hair brushed back from a heavy-featured face, olive skin, and a body the size of a tank. "Maybe the three hundred pounds didn't exactly lend itself to coronary health."

"Watch it." Sandy ceased her typing. "I know what it feels like to have a butt the size of the Gulf of Mexico."

"Hardly."

"Well . . . maybe only Lake Okeechobee, but it used to take twenty minutes every morning to squeeze myself into size fourteen pants." She shuddered. "I still can't believe I'm a size ten now."

"Okay, back to Mr. Santini. Anything on the autopsy yet?"

"Nope."

"Who found the body?"

"His niece, Beatrice."

"Jeez . . . that must've been a shock." I shuddered myself as I remembered what it felt like to find a dead body. I'd had a couple of incidents like that since coming to Coral Island, none of them pleasant. "Forget about the official story—what's the island grapevine got to say about the death?"

Sandy paused and leaned back in her chair. "Everyone is sort of cut up about it. Mr. Santini was a great guy. He ran the ice cream shop at the island center, did a lot of volunteer work at the soup kitchen, and never had a harsh word to say about anyone—"

"Oh, I remember him now." I snapped my fingers. "I used to stop in his store sometimes after work for a double scoop of rum walnut ice cream—if I wanted to skip dinner. And he always gave me extra toppings at no charge. Great guy. I'm so sorry to hear about his death." I sighed. "He really wasn't that out of shape to have a massive heart attack—just stocky."

She leveled a long, silent glance at me.

I stared back. "What are you saying?"

"Carlos Santini's brother, Marco, hated him—always had, but it really got worse the last six months."

"Why?"

"Marco's daughter, Beatrice. She began dating an exchange student from Italy who works in the restaurant. A nice kid. But Marco has done everything to break them up. If you ask me, he's just plain mean." She shook her head. "I guess the two brothers had a big argument at the restaurant the day before Santini was found dead."

"You think there was . . . foul play?"

Sandy shrugged.

"Right. Let me call Nick." I picked up my cell phone and speed dialed him, my heart beating a little faster.

"Nick Billie here," his deep voice answered on the first ring.

"Hi, this is Mallie. I've got a couple of questions about Carlos Santini's death—"

"The autopsy isn't back yet," he cut in with a clipped tone.

"When did Beatrice find the body?" I cradled my cell between my ear and shoulder as I pulled out my reporter's notepad. My radar was up; something seemed off about this whole thing.

"Yesterday morning. She had stopped by Santini's house and found him in his recliner—he was sitting in front of the TV with a glass of wine at his side."

"Alone?" I scribbled down a few notes that I probably wouldn't be able to decipher later.

"Uh-huh."

"Do you think—"

"There's nothing unusual about his death." I could hear his deep sigh. "I've got someone with me right now. I'll call you later." He clicked off.

I stuck my tongue out at the cell phone and then snapped it shut.

"What did Nick say?" Sandy queried.

"Not much." My tone must have said it all, because she didn't probe any further. "What's Marco Santini like?"

"The opposite of Carlos in every way. Tall, thin—and kind of snippy. Jimmy told me that Marco runs a tight ship at the restaurant, which is probably why Beatrice spent so much time with her uncle. She has to work for her father all day at Little Tuscany."

Jimmy had moved from painter to waitstaff after he got engaged—a good move. During tourist season, he made almost a hundred bucks a night in tips.

"Sounds more like Little Terrorsville," I murmured, still irritated over Nick's abrupt dismissal. I might have been known as "Mixed-up Mallie" for the first twenty years of my life, but I now had a job (semi-permanent), a home (the Airstream in an RV park), and two boyfriends (maybe only one now), and I deserved better than the "official island cop" blow-off. "Back to Carlos—anything else I need to know?"

"Well, he stayed single, so Beatrice was more like the daughter that he never had," Sandy continued in a soft voice. "That's about it. I guess that I'll make sure to get a quote from her for the obit."

"Fitting." I grabbed my hobo bag—a new addition to my wardrobe since my ten-year-old veteran bag split at the seams from all the junk I carried around. This one had double reinforced seams and a peace sign embroidered on the front. I tossed in a few pens and a small spiral-bound notebook. Then I tossed in two chocolate bars. "Much as I want to find out more about Carlos' death, I can't put off Le Sink any longer." I printed out the directions and stuffed that inside the hobo bag too.

"Good luck!"

"I think I'll need it—"

The front door of the newspaper office suddenly whipped open, and Madame Geri stood at the entrance, an alarmed expression on her face. "The wedding is off!"

Sandy looked up, her eyes widening in shock. "What?"

"All plans are canceled because a killer is loose."

My hobo bag slid to the floor with a thump, and Sandy let out a small shriek.

Oh my god. Was Carlos Santini murdered?

Chapter Two

I ... don't understand," Sandy stammered, panic in her voice.

Madame Geri held up her arms, chanted a few words in a low tone, then fastened her glance on Sandy. "It's confirmed by the spirit world: a killer is on the island, and your wedding plans will be canceled whether you like it or not."

Sandy opened her mouth and tried to formulate a few words, but nothing came out. Then her eyes filled with tears, and her shoulders began to shake.

"All right, let's stop all of this alarmist talk," I interjected as I moved around my desk to stand behind Sandy. Patting her on the shoulder, I glared at Madame Geri, like a tigress protecting her cub—even though Sandy was technically around my age. "I don't think pseudocommunication from some kind of phony spirit world qualifies as a reason for Sandy to call off her wedding. For goodness' sake, she's marrying *your* son."

Madame Geri raised her chin and tossed back her

blond dreadlocks. "I'm well aware of that, but one does not challenge the spirit world." She smoothed down her fifties retro white cotton dress embroidered with tiny red apples. Middle-aged but with smooth, unlined skin, Madame Geri had the look of the Mad Housewife generation with a touch of Bob Marley: preppy-boho-loony chic.

Sandy cried harder. "I can't go through with it now. If I try, Jimmy and I will be cursed and never have a moment's peace."

"That's ridiculous," I spat out. "Why would the possibility of a *killer* on the island affect your wedding plans?" I rolled my eyes in skepticism at Madame Geri.

"M-maybe he's targeting Jimmy or me," Sandy managed to get out between sobs. "We can't get married if one of us is d-dead."

"Stop it!" I cut in swiftly. "Madame Geri didn't say anything about you or Jimmy dying. You're jumping to conclusions over some half-baked prediction—"

"Now you stop it." It was Madame Geri's turn to cut in, with a warning glance leveled in my direction. "The spirit world never lies to me. Something is going to happen that will end the wedding plans, but it won't be Sandy's or Jimmy's death."

"Okay, that sounds a little better." I gave a halfhearted nod in Madame Geri's direction, trying to reassure myself that Nick had said nothing appeared suspicious about Santini's death.

Sandy stopped crying.

"So neither of you is in danger of actually dying," I continued in an upbeat tone.

"Of course not," Madame Geri agreed. "It's the wedding that's in danger—of not happening."

Sandy began crying again.

"Can we have a reality check here?" I said, throwing up my hands in frustration. I'd received "messages" from Madame Geri's spirit world before, and they were always vague. My contention was, if spirits were going to communicate with those of us still on planet Earth, you'd think they would find a way to give concrete advice like "Don't wear red—it clashes with your hair." Or, "Don't run that stop sign—a cop is hiding behind those trees." Or, "Don't major in comparative literature—you'll never get a decent job." That was the type of advice I wish I had heard. If I had been treated to a few of those little suggestions during my life, things might have turned out differently.

"The spirit world doesn't communicate the way the living do—they live on a different plane of existence," Madame Geri pronounced, as if reading my thoughts. "And redheads *can* wear red."

Okay, now she was freaking me out.

"What am I going to do?" Sandy wailed.

"That depends on Mallie," Madame Geri chimed in, pointing at me. "*You* might be able to avert the disaster."

"Me? How?" I started thinking about Mr. Santini again.

"You need to start investigating anything out of the ordinary on the island. Something has already been set into motion, and you're the one who can figure it out."

"Like . . . a suspicious death?" A warning light flickered inside of me.

"Maybe." Madame Geri closed her eyes again for a few brief moments. "All I get is 'pasta.' It has something to do with pasta."

"Huh?" I asked, knitting my brows. "What does it mean?"

Madame Geri shrugged. "I'm only transmitting what they tell me."

"What type of pasta?" I persisted. "Macaroni? Spaghetti? Ziti?"

"I don't know," she said, raising one eyebrow and enunciating each word with annoyed emphasis.

Sandy opened her desk drawer and fished out a Hershey's mini chocolate bar and chewed with a meditative expression. "Okay, let's think what the spirit world might mean by pasta being a barrier to my marriage. We don't eat a lot of pasta, so it must have something to do with Jimmy's job at Little Tuscany, where he *serves* pasta." Sandy's eyes widened with dawning realization, and her hand went to her mouth. "That's it! Marco Santini owns the restaurant—maybe he killed his brother with pasta. What do you think, Mallie?"

"I don't think you can actually *kill* someone with pasta," I said. Just talking about carbohydrates made me hungry, though this spirit world thing also creeped me out.

"What are you two talking about?" Madame Geri looked from Sandy to me, and then back at Sandy. "Was someone murdered?"

"Yes!" Sandy exclaimed.

"No!" I burst out. "Well, maybe. We're not sure. The circumstances of his death seemed a little odd, but Nick Billie said that there was nothing suspicious about it, and I believe him. Still, the way that Mr. Santini died—at home in his recliner . . . it makes me uneasy." My motor-mouth had kicked in with a savage acceleration—a sure sign of inward anxiety. Some people get sweaty palms or stutter; I just talk on and on and on. "I hate to say this, but I get a funny feeling—"

"That's it." Madame Geri reached into her little square purse and pulled out a cell phone.

"Are you calling Nick?" I reached for one of Sandy's Hershey's bars.

She flashed me an insincere grin. "No, I'm making a reservation for lunch at Little Tuscany. We need to check it out."

"Oh, no—"

"Oh, *yes*," Anita chimed in from the doorway of her office. "That's a perfect restaurant to begin your food critic blog, kiddo—especially if it could lead to a bigger story of murder and mayhem."

"Were you eavesdropping?" I asked with some indignation as I downed the chocolate.

"Duh—like that's hard to do with my paper-thin walls. I've been listening to this twaddle for the last ten minutes. Pure bunk! But then again, if there's even a chance to stir up some drama for the paper, I can't pass it up."

I opened my mouth to protest but then realized that I wouldn't have to go to Le Sink after all. My mouth clamped shut.

"You can visit Le Sink for dinner," Anita added. "Oh, I just thought of something else—hit Pelican's Grill for a second dinner. They buy a buttload of advertising with us."

Damn.

"Hey, I got to go with my gut—it's served me well in the past when I worked at the *Detroit Free Press.*" Anita folded her arms across her skinny chest, with a smug expression. "But now, my face might be my fortune too, on account of the bee cream. I think I'm starting to look like a hottie."

I peered at her skin. "Anita, your skin is all red from that stuff."

She patted her cheeks and arms. "For now. Then it's going to peel, and my skin will look as smooth as a baby's bottom."

When pigs fly.

"Bee pollen from this island doesn't agree with human skin," Madame Geri warned. "You won't like the results."

"Says you." Anita gave a scoffing laugh and disappeared back into her cubicle.

Madame Geri shook her head. "She's going to look like a broiled lobster in a day or two. It won't be pretty."

"It wasn't pretty to begin with." I gave Sandy a little pat on the shoulder. "Don't worry, sweetie, we'll find out if there's anything out of the ordinary going on at Little Tuscany. You and Jimmy are meant to be together, and we're not going to let a possible killer stand in the way of your wedding."

"Thanks, Mallie." A little tremor lingered in her voice. "I'm counting on you and Madame Geri. I've spent a ton of money on the wedding already, and I've literally dieted my buns off to look good in my white dress." She bit her lip. "Not to mention, if Marco murdered his brother, he should be brought to justice."

"And then your wedding can go forward," I added with an encouraging smile.

"Sandy, have a fallback plan—just in case." Madame Geri tossed her cell phone back into her purse. "You and Jimmy can always just live together if things don't work out."

"Mercy me." Sandy buried her head in her hands.

I just glared at Madame Geri.

After we both settled into my ancient truck, Rusty (named for obvious reasons), I turned on Madame Geri. "Do you think you could be a little more positive? This wedding is Sandy's big moment, and you're ruining it for her."

"*Au contraire.*" She folded her hands in her lap, the

ornate silver bracelets on both wrists making a delicate tinkling sound. "I'm trying to make certain her wedding takes place. But when I know negative forces are at work, we have to act. That's the only way to avoid a potential disaster."

"Whatever." I cranked the key, and nothing happened. I pumped the pedal with a series of short taps and turned the key again. Rusty's engine sputtered, spewed a blast of exhaust, and eventually started up.

Madame Geri coughed as the fumes wafted through Rusty's open windows. She started to roll up her passenger side window, but I halted her efforts by letting her know that my air-conditioning was on the fritz again.

"Maybe you should get a new vehicle," she pointed out, waving her hand in front of her face in an attempt to clear the air.

"Sure, whenever you can persuade Anita to give me a raise. In case you haven't noticed, I'm not exactly making CEO wages." I backed the truck out of the parking space, looking over my shoulder, since the rearview mirror had fallen off for the umpteenth time.

"Maybe I'll ask someone to talk with her on your behalf," she said.

"Who? Benton?" I scoffed. "He's just as much of a cheapo."

She shook her head.

"Bernice? Her evil twin sister?"

She pursed her lips.

I glanced at her in puzzlement, and then realization

flooded through me. "No, don't tell me that you're going through a spirit world contact—"

"Why not? Even Anita must've had a relative who gave her guidance in this life but has moved on to the great beyond."

"More likely she was created in a laboratory somewhere like Dr. Frankenstein's monster—the 'hideous progeny.'"

"We'll see." She closed her eyes and mumbled a few inaudible words.

"Don't do that!" I shouted as I turned onto Cypress Road—the island's main drag—and rammed down the gas pedal. Rusty promptly accelerated to thirty-five mph. "I don't want any dead-person cooties lingering in my truck." I tapped the gas pedal again, but Rusty only eked up to forty-five miles per hour. *Just peachy.* I wanted Madame Geri and any remnants of Anita's spectral ancestors out of my truck—pronto.

Madame Geri opened her eyes. "I'm not getting anything. That's odd."

"I told you—Anita isn't human."

"Of course she is, but it's odd that no one from the spirit world will come forward to connect with her."

"Really? Would *you* want to spend one minute of your afterlife thinking about Anita Sanders?" I drove with one hand, lifting my hair from the back of my neck with the other hand, trying vainly to keep cool.

"Everyone has a lovable side. Even Anita." She leaned back against the tattered headrest. "But I don't get the lack

of response from the spirit world. Oh, well, I'll keep trying until I figure it out, especially if "—she paused—"you
want that new truck."

"Well . . . uh . . . go for it." I gave her a thumbs-up.
But, in truth, much as I would like a new vehicle with an
air conditioner and windows that went up and down, I
wasn't sure if I could part ways with Rusty. My old truck
had seen me through some rough spots, like when we
towed my four-thousand-pound Airstream through the
Appalachian Mountains. Rusty gave all his muscle on the
way up (barely eked out twenty-five miles per hour) and
showed what he was made of on the way down (burned
out the brakes). Could a new truck do that? I wasn't sure.

"I guess new isn't always better," Madame Geri commented.

Yikes. She did it again—read my mind. *Double freaky.*

Gritting my teeth, I didn't respond—just focused on
the road.

We drove the rest of the way in silence, as the tropical
scenery whizzed past. Despite its being October, the
temperature still hovered near the upper eighties, and
everything appeared lush and green—from the delicate
palm fronds to the sharp-edged saw palmetto stalks.

A cold spell was supposed to be on the way, but you
couldn't tell it from the midday, energy-sucking heat. I
still hadn't gotten used to the lack of autumn in Florida
with its vividly colored landscape, but in January, when
the rest of the country was up to its wazoo in snow, I
loved it.

Heading south, I flipped open my cell phone and dialed Cole. He didn't pick up, so I left him a voice mail to say that we'd be dining at Le Sink tonight. Of my two quasi boyfriends, he was the one to take to a low-scale restaurant; nothing ever fazed him. Blond with surfer good looks, he also possessed a laid-back, life's-a-beach outlook. Our relationship was fun, carefree, and pleasant.

Everything a girl could want—sort of.

"You need more than a guy who looks good on a surfboard," Madame Geri commented, trying to keep cool by leaning her head as far out the window as she possibly could without being decapitated.

"I don't want to talk about my personal life." I flipped my cell phone shut with deliberate force, hoping she would get the nonverbal reinforcement.

"Suit yourself, but he's not the one for you. There's no getting around it—you're a different woman from the one who first came to Coral Island, and he can't give you what you need."

I gripped the steering wheel tighter but said nothing. Was it because she had touched on the truth? Or because of her smug, all-knowing air? Or maybe it was because the wheel had started to shimmy like a hula dancer, which it often did when Rusty accelerated over fifty miles per hour.

"Be careful—"

"Just let me drive, will you?" At that moment, an elderly guy turned in front of me on his three-wheel bicycle. I rammed on the brakes, and Rusty screeched to a halt, brakes squealing and worn rubber tires burning. Madame Geri and I both jerked forward and then backward as the seat belts kicked in.

I blinked and exhaled a shaky breath. "Whew, that was a close call."

"I tried to warn you." Madame Geri grasped the passenger door to steady herself. "I could feel the red energy blitzing my brain—that always means danger ahead."

"Thanks for the tip." I was too upset to argue with her.

The old guy just waved in a friendly gesture as he pedaled with turtlelike speed to the other side of the road. I started to curse at him; then he flashed a smile in my direction, revealing two missing teeth and a mean overbite. I waved back.

"Oh no." Madame Geri had her glance fastened on the passenger-side mirror. I looked over my shoulder and saw flashing blue lights. *Oh no, indeed.* It was the island police. I prayed that it wasn't Nick Billie; the last thing I needed was for him to see me almost hit an aging, toothless man on a tricycle.

I pulled over and came to a halt, though I didn't dare turn off the engine in case Rusty wouldn't restart. Then I spied the tall, trim form of Nick Billie. *Double oh no.*

"Hi, Nick." I propped my arm on the open window and looked up at him with a bright smile, forgetting my earlier irritation over his official-island-cop attitude. To be honest, his hunky presence always caused my mind to blank out and my heart to beat faster than a race car in overdrive—or than Rusty's engine when the gears were slipping. *Hottie* didn't even begin to describe his handsome, hard-planed face, deep brown eyes, and jet black hair. More like *sizzling*.

I hoped that he would attribute my flushed face to the heat.

"Hello." He inclined his head in Madame Geri's direction. She responded with the same gesture.

"You know, I didn't mean to almost hit the biking geriatric," I started in with a preemptive explanation. "He turned in front of me with no warning, no hand signal, nothing. So, I did what I could to avoid hitting him, as you could see. But I don't want to be ticketed for reckless driving, since I was barely doing fifty in a sixty-mile-per-hour zone." Needless to say, the motormouth had kicked in once again.

"I saw the whole thing," he cut in, swiping his sweaty forehead with the back of his hand. "Before you get up too much of a head of steam, that isn't why I pulled you over."

Had he "blue-lighted" me because he was regretting his clipped tone in our phone conversation earlier? Or was it because we hadn't seen each other in over a week, and he missed me so much that he pretended I had a traffic violation?

"I noticed when you stopped that your left brake light is out."

Oh.

"You need to get that fixed ASAP," he continued. "I have a friend at Palm Auto who can replace the bulb for you."

"Thanks." I struggled to summon a degree of enthusiasm over the brake bulb. I guess it was thoughtful, but not exactly the kind of gesture that made a girl want to swoon.

He cleared his throat. "I also wanted to know if you'd like to have dinner with me tonight . . . to discuss adding some new 'Police Beat' items for the *Observer* this week—"

"Mr. Santini's death?" My breath caught in my throat.

He dropped his head and groaned.

"Hey, there's nothing like a little death conversation to liven up dinner," I offered.

Nick gave a short bark of laughter and then raised his head. "All right. I'm working a double shift today, so can I meet you around eight?"

"Pelican's Grill?" *Heh.* I could knock out the restaurant review at the same time—if I could focus on the food.

"It's a date."

Okay, so the dinner was work-related; it *felt* like a date.

He flipped one of my curls and grinned. "You'd better believe it." Tipping a jaunty little salute at Madame Geri, he strode back to his F-150 truck and slipped the light off the roof. Then he hung a U-turn and headed in the opposite direction. *Wow.* Sleek and powerful, the midnight-colored truck reflected its owner—dark and sexy. I might not like to self-analyze before (or after) lunch, but my vehicular psychoanalysis of others gave me great insights to human nature. My theory was that people generally drove the kind of auto that reflected their personality: Rusty the Truck spoke volumes about me, including my lack of substantial amounts of cash to afford a new mode of transport or even perform basic maintenance.

Humming under my breath, I steered Rusty back onto Cypress Drive. A date with Nick Billie. *Fabu.*

"I think you forgot something," Madame Geri interjected.

I blinked. "What?"

"You just called Cole to have dinner with you at Le Sink." She leveled an amused glance in my direction. "I don't need to contact the spirit world to know that you've double-booked yourself."

Twenty minutes later, we arrived at Little Tuscany. I'd spent most of the remaining drive hatching schemes with Madame Geri on how I could manage to make both of my commitments tonight. After several possible scenarios, I proposed that I would meet Cole at Le Sink around six p.m. Then I'd say that I had to go back to work to write the restaurant review on the *Observer* blog. After I managed to escape early by telling that tiny, tiny white lie, I'd hightail it to Pelican's Grill for my dinner date with Nick and pump him for info about Mr. Santini. It could work . . . I just knew it.

"Not telling the truth is bad karma," Madame Geri stated flatly. "No good will come of it."

"Says you." I parked Rusty and hopped out before she could say anything else. I didn't want to hear it. After almost a two-year man drought, I finally had two guys in tow on the same night. What could be better?

Madame Geri appeared at my side, her mouth set in a thin line. I ignored that too.

"Don't worry, I know what I'm doing. Let's get some lunch and see if we can question Marco Santini." I marched toward the entrance of Little Tuscany, a small-ish one-story stucco building painted a deep shade of pink with yellow shutters. Someone had outlined a map of Italy to the left of the front door, but whoever sketched it wasn't exactly Picasso, because instead of resembling a boot, the country looked like a skinny leg with a flip-flop.

A bad omen? Or just bad art?

We entered, and after taking in a lovely breath of cool air, I noticed the faux Italy atmosphere throughout, from the mural of ancient Rome on the back wall—complete with a portrait of some muscular guy in a toga—to the olive oil bottles, the smell of garlic, and, finally, some un-identified warbler's version of "Volare." Maybe this wasn't such a step up from Le Sink. More like *Le Fake*.

Still, the crowded, noisy dining room meant the food was probably good.

"Mom!" Jimmy sprinted toward us from the bar area. "Sandy just called me to say our wedding might be can-celed because of a *killer!*"

Instantly, everyone stopped speaking, and all eyes focused on us.

"It's a joke." I waved my hands in dissent to everyone and then pointed at Jimmy and offered the group an apologetic smile. "He's a nervous groom, having some last-minute jitters. Everything is fine. Just fine. No murder."

Jimmy's beefy face crinkled in puzzlement. "But I thought—"

"Why don't you show us to a table?" I suggested, pinching Madame Geri's arm so she wouldn't contradict me. The last thing we needed was the island on red alert before we had any concrete evidence of murder.

Eventually, the conversation started up again, but I could tell from some of the furtive glances in our direction that not everyone bought my reassurances.

"Uh, I'm not allowed to seat the guests. Mr. Marco is the maître d'." His voice dropped almost a whisper. "He'll kick my butt if I try to do his job."

"Nonsense." Madame Geri spoke up. "I see a great spot over by the ruins of the Forum." She sauntered in the direction of a table by the mural.

"Stop right there!" a man shouted.

Madame Geri kept going, but the diners ceased speaking again—this time in curious anticipation.

"Don't you *dare* take that table!" he yelled out like a sonic boom.

I watched as a string-bean-thin middle-aged guy sporting an apron and bad comb-over charged across the room like a train heading for the station. Then Madame Geri made herself known by slowly turning around. He stopped in his tracks.

"Dio mio." He clutched the menus to his chest and crossed himself as if he'd committed a major sin.

"Madame Geri, I'm so sorry. I didn't realize it was you. I don't think we've ever met formally, but I'm Marco Santini—owner of Little Tuscany. Please, choose the table that suits you. I'm so sorry. So sorry. Take any table. If someone is already seated there, I'll move them."

The patrons murmured among themselves, some even taking out their wallets or purses to pay, no doubt readying themselves to move for the island's freelance psychic. *Unbelievable.*

I eyed Marco. He didn't appear to be a killer—more like an aging car salesman.

"No need." She motioned Jimmy over. "My son said this one was the best seat in the house."

"Jimmy is *your* son?" A shadow of anxiety passed across his face. He obviously was trying to remember if he'd done anything to Jimmy that would incur Madame Geri's wrath.

Madame Geri nodded, a proud mother's smile spreading across her face.

"I'm at your service. Whatever you need, please let me know." He gave a little bow, but his breathing seemed to be coming in short gasps, belying his smooth assurances. "Jimmy will be your waiter—unless you'd prefer to have him *join* you for lunch. In that case, I'd be happy to assign one of my other waitstaff to your table."

"I'd prefer Jimmy as our waiter." She gave Marco a flick of an eyebrow, which he interpreted as dismissal.

After setting the menus on the table, he backed away from her and quickly disappeared into the kitchen.

"He's probably hanging garlic around his neck in case you're putting a curse on him," I commented as I seated myself.

"Like that would help," Madame Geri scoffed, sliding into a chair opposite mine. "We'll talk to Mr. Marco after we eat lunch; that way, I'll get the right vibe to see if he killed his brother—"

"Carlos?" Jimmy's mouth dropped open. "You don't think that Mr. Marco—"

"We don't know anything for sure," I cut in swiftly, keeping my tone calm. "But we're here to dig around."

Madame Geri nodded. "So you can still get married, Jimmy—"

"Thanks, Mom." Jimmy leaned down and gave her a quick hug. "I love Sandy so much, and I really want to marry her."

"Now, my dear, the wedding may not take place the way you've planned it," she said gently. "But I'll try and find a way for it still to happen."

"Uh . . . well . . ." He hesitated until his mother patted him on the arm. "Okay, I'll call Sandy and give her some encouragement before she eats every Hershey's bar on the island." He started to leave, then glanced back at us. "What would you like to drink?"

"We'll have unsweetened iced teas," Madame Geri said as I started to mouth "a beer."

Jimmy strode away from the table before I could correct her. "I may need something stronger if this day keeps going the way it started," I hissed at my lunch companion.

"You need to keep your wits about you if you're going to do the restaurant review." She handed me a menu. "And find out what caused Carlos' death."

I weighed Madame Geri with a critical squint, knowing she was right; I had to know if there truly was a killer loose on Coral Island—especially if Jimmy's matrimonial future might be hanging in the balance. Sighing at the responsibility looming ahead of me, I flipped open the menu and scanned through the massive number of appetizers and entrées. Spaghetti, ravioli, ziti—this was pasta haven.

"If *pasta* is the word that the spirit world gave you, we're in the right place to find out what they meant. I've never seen so many different pasta dishes." *But no fried anything,* I added to myself. *Shoot.*

Madame Geri looked around, taking in the tacky Tuscany atmosphere. "We're in the right place; I can feel it. I don't like the vibes. Something is off." She shivered.

Now it was my turn to be nervous. I'd never seen Madame Geri's feathers even slightly ruffled by anything—even talking to dead people. Of course, her son hadn't been involved, so that might be putting a new spin on the spirit world's wacky predictions.

Jimmy returned with our iced teas, and we each ordered a pasta dish—hers primavera, mine spaghetti and meatballs. Marco had also reappeared, but he lingered at the bar, pretending not to watch us as he fidgeted with the strings of his apron. Why was he so agitated?

Did he have something to hide?

"Sandy seemed a little better after I talked to her," Jimmy commented, as he placed a small bowl of sliced limes and lemons on our table. "I wasn't sure which one you liked for your tea, so I brought both."

"I'm a lime girl." I squeezed a hearty amount of its liquid into my tea, but it squirted out in several directions—both Madame Geri and her son winced and then rubbed their eyes.

"Sorry—guess the lime juice has a mind of its own." I cupped my hand around the second slice to restrict its acidic stream. "So, Jimmy, has there been anything unusual going on here lately?" I stole a few more glimpses in Marco's direction.

He paused. "Not really—just business as usual."

"Is your boss treating you right?" Madame Geri asked. "He seemed a little . . . belligerent." She enunciated every syllable of the last word and glanced over in Marco's direction. He responded with a shaky smile and disappeared again into the kitchen.

"Mom, he's not *that* bad," Jimmy commented, still trying to clear his vision from the lime-juice spritz. "Mr. Santini might be kind of a nitpicker in the kitchen, but I can't believe he'd harm his own brother. Granted, he hasn't taken it too hard, but he and Carlos didn't get along too well." He blinked a couple more times. "Poor Beatrice, though—she's pretty cut up over her uncle's death. She's been sobbing all day."

"Can't say I blame her," I chimed in. "Nick Billie told me that Beatrice found his body in a recliner—"

"We need to talk to Marco—now," Madame Geri interrupted. "The vibes are getting worse."

Oh, jeez.

Jimmy gulped. "I'll go get him—"

All of a sudden, Marco's shouting could be heard from the kitchen. "I told you *not* to chop the carrots like that, you idiot!"

"I'm sorry, Mr. Marco," a younger man's pleading voice wafted out. "I won't do it again."

"You're damn right you won't—you're fired!"

"I'll have to go back to Italy if I lose my job," the other man said, his voice rising in volume. "You can't do that to me and Beatrice."

"Yes, I *can!* You don't have Carlos here anymore to coddle you."

"Put the knife down, Papa," a female voice pleaded.

Knife?

My eyes met Madame Geri's in alarm.

The kitchen door burst open, and a slim, dark-haired, young Italian stallion dashed out, Marco in his wake; the latter held up a large butcher knife in his hand.

The diners ceased conversation for a third time to watch the show.

"Stay away from my Beatrice!" Marco pointed the

knife at him, his breath coming in short gasps. "You're not good enough for her—I've told you that again and again. Now, get out, and don't come back."

The young man held his ground, but I could see his hands trembling as he faced down the knife. I'd be running for my life, though I hadn't exactly done that when a murderer threatened me with a paint knife (but that's another story).

"I'd better separate them," Jimmy said, starting in that direction, but Madame Geri grabbed his arm.

"No! Call the police." She pulled out her cell phone and handed it to him.

Before he could punch in the number, Marco continued with his tirade: "Get out, you loser! I'm not saying it again." He advanced toward the younger man, raising the knife over his head.

"Stop it, right now!" I screamed, as I pushed back my chair and stood up. *Where did that come from?*

Both men turned and looked at me.

"You're . . . uh, ruining everyone's lunch." That was lame, but it was the best I could come up with. My knees shook as if I had palsy.

"Leave Guido alone!" another diner yelled. "He's a good kid."

A chorus of agreement echoed around the dining room.

Marco lowered the knife and put a hand to his head, swaying back and forth. "I . . . I don't feel well."

The knife dropped to the floor with a thud; then he

began to wheeze and cough but managed to stay on his feet. "I can't b-breathe."

With his face turning red and blotchy, he clawed at his throat.

"Call 911!" I yelled, sprinting across the room—just in time to see Marco topple over and Guido catch him. They both sank to the floor.

Marco gulped for air, his whole body shuddering.

By the time I got to his side, he wasn't moving.

"Quick, try CPR!" I exclaimed.

Guido quickly complied. After several minutes of breathing into Marco's mouth and pumping his chest, the young man leaned back, tears in his eyes. "I don't think it will help."

No, it wouldn't.

Marco was dead.

Chapter Three

Silence descended on the diners like a heavy blanket of darkness at the sudden appearance of death's shadow. No one moved; no one spoke.

I cleared my throat, and as if on cue, everyone began shouting and yelling on cell phones in unison.

In the midst of the total chaos, I sank to my knees next to Guido, not sure what to do. "Where are those damn paramedics?" I grabbed Marco's hand, frantically trying to get a pulse.

It felt cold, without a detectable heartbeat. Then I felt the side of his neck. Nothing. A mute cry of sadness rose up in my throat.

Tears slid down Guido's face. "I tried, I tried," he kept repeating as he rocked back and forth on the floor next to me.

"What's going on?" A young woman appeared in the kitchen doorway, her delicate, cameolike face knit with concern and confusion.

"Beatrice!" someone exclaimed. "Stay in the kitchen."

But when she spied Guido and me on the floor, she raced over and then halted, her mouth dropping open in shock. "Papa!"

She threw herself on top of Marco, shaking him by the shoulders. "What's wrong with him? Why isn't he moving?"

After a few moments, she burst into sobs and buried her face in her father's chest—her long brown hair spilling over both of them like a shield.

Just then, I heard sirens—and the paramedics appeared seconds later.

"Stand back, please," one man said in a deep, firm voice, as he gently eased Beatrice away from her father. I quickly moved out of the way.

They tried everything to bring life back into Marco—CPR, injections, heart paddles—but nothing worked. He just lay there, totally unresponsive.

"I'm sorry, ma'am, but there's nothing we can do," the paramedic said to Beatrice, who then crumpled into Guido's arms. "He probably had anaphylaxis—an extreme allergic reaction to something."

"Papa!" she exclaimed, clinging to Guido. They cried together, and I found my own eyes welling up. How could Marco have expired in front of us so quickly from an allergy? Was it possible?

I sensed Madame Geri at my elbow, and I sort of sagged into her briefly. For some reason, right now I found her familiar patchouli perfume presence comforting.

The paramedics wheeled Marco out, and Beatrice followed with Guido practically carrying her, tears still streaming down her cheeks. After they left, everyone turned deadly quiet yet again. People just milled around— not sure whether they should leave.

After a few minutes, Jimmy motioned the customers toward the front door, "We'd better close the restaurant, everyone—and please don't worry about paying your bill. Our apologies."

All of the diners filed out of the restaurant with a somber silence, leaving Madame Geri, Jimmy, and me. The kitchen staff hovered near the back door, and Jimmy nodded in their direction. They left too.

"Well . . . that was unbelievable—and sad," I commented to no one in particular. "Poor Marco."

Jimmy shook his head. "Terrible."

"I probably shouldn't be asking this question, but what about Carlos' death?" I continued.

"Who can say for sure?" Madame Geri interjected in a soft voice. "I wish I could say or do more, but that's life and death—as I learned when Jimmy's father died. Believe me, if I could have stopped *that,* I would have, but the events were bigger than my powers—it's destiny."

My eyes widened. I'd never heard Madame Geri talk like that. "I . . . I didn't know."

"Now you do." Her chin tilted higher, and a flutter of sorrow winged across her face, tugging at my already jumbled emotions. All of a sudden, we both started to weep.

"All right, time to go," Jimmy said, ushering us out of

there while we blubbered, and he locked the restaurant behind us.

An hour later, I parked Rusty in front of my Airstream and sat there, savoring the comforting sight of my 4,220-pound RV with its gleaming silver exterior and blue-and-white striped awning.

Ah. Nirvana.

It never failed to restore me—even in the wake of trauma.

I pushed the day's events out of my mind as I beheld my little spot at the Twin Palms RV Resort, which edged on Coral Island's only beach, or what passes for a beach around here: a tiny strip of sand that almost disappears when the tide comes in. But I loved it—the salty air, sea breeze, and rolling waves. Unfortunately, the island stretches north–south and is enclosed by the more popular, touristy barrier islands with their wide beaches, so this bit of sandy shore was about it.

I looked over to the van positioned on the left of my Airstream—that's where Cole was housed. He'd driven the vehicle all over the West "trying to find himself," and the van looked like it had seen some hard road. My degree in Automotive Psychology from *Car and Driver* magazine told me his van-home reflected his lifestyle: free and simple. I liked that—kind of.

Then I checked out the site to my right. For a moment, I thought I saw the outlines of another Airstream.

Smaller, shabbier, but with the same silver, hutlike appearance. Then I blinked, and it was gone. The site was empty.

Must've been glare from the sun.

"Cole?"

No answer. He was probably on a shoot—his freelance photography job provided enough money for his site at the RV resort, food, and an endless supply of boogie boards to skim the surf.

I sighed. At one time, I would have found that combination fun and attractive. But, now, after all my experiences on the island—including murder and mayhem—I might have become (gasp) more serious about life. *Possibly.* But every time I was with Cole, I thought about Nick, and every time I was with Nick, I thought about Cole. I had officially become indecisive and two-faced.

A tiny scratching sound caught my attention. Kong. I made for my Airstream door and swung it open to behold my teacup poodle standing there, his tail flipping back and forth in excitement to see me.

"Hi, sweet pea." He licked my ankle.

Now, what man could compete with that?

I grabbed his leash, hooked it onto his collar, and we made for the surf. He trotted alongside me, sniffing the briny air and perking up his ears at the sound of the seabirds diving for fish. As we reached the shoreline, though, he put the brakes on. Kong hated water—especially salt water. He loved the beach, but he didn't like getting wet.

"Come on, Kong, cut me some slack." I yanked at his leash. "I've had a really rotten day, I've got two dinner dates tonight, and I'll probably need to stay up until all hours writing the restaurant reviews when I get home."

He barked in response but didn't move. I gave the leash another tug, but for a minuscule little pup, he could be amazingly strong. Ever since I had taken him to a doggy psychologist to help him get over his inferiority complex regarding his diminutive size and named him King Kong—Kong for short (no pun intended)—he took great pride in asserting himself at the most inopportune moments.

Karma. You fix one thing, and it causes something else.

"All right. Get it in gear." I yanked on the leash and strode over to a clump of palmetto palms. After staring at me for a few moments in defiance, he finally started to lift his leg—

"Mallie!" a female voice yelled out.

Distracted, Kong immediately dropped his leg, and I groaned in frustration.

"Did I interrupt him?" Wanda Sue, my landlady, asked as she strolled toward me.

"No, of course not." I summoned a halfhearted smile, but it widened into a real grin as I took in Wanda Sue's outfit. Middle-aged and fighting every minute of it, she wore neon blue spandex shorts, a low-cut cotton top with the neckline decorated in feathers, and cheap gold dangling earrings—also with feathers on the ends.

The only thing missing was a headdress perched on her bouffant hairdo. Of course, I wasn't sure that a headdress would exactly fit on hair teased that high, but if anyone could do it, it was Wanda Sue.

She owned the Twin Palms RV Resort and had been my dear friend since I arrived on Coral Island. Warm, caring, and a fashionista dropout, she had taken me under her fleshy wing from the first day. She was also plugged into the Coral Island gossip network and knew if a car so much as backfired within a ten-mile radius. Needless to say, the latter talent helped me enormously when I was working on a particularly difficult news story.

"So, honey, what in tarnation happened at Little Tuscany?" she asked. Wanda Sue also had a southern drawl as deep and thick as the Everglades.

"You've already heard?" Okay, it was a rhetorical question, but I had to ask.

"Oh, Mallie." She waved a hand bejeweled with rings. "I heard from Pop Pop, who heard it from the Jordan twins, who got it from their mother at the Island Hardware store, who got it from her neighbor who was having lunch at Little Tuscany when it happened."

Whew. Talk about a grapevine; that one could choke an elephant.

"Did Marco die of an allergic reaction?" she continued, leaning down to pat Kong on the head. He growled and then stomped on her foot with his little paw.

"Sweet little pooch."

Undaunted, Kong raised his ears and barked again.

"Sorry. He's a little cranky from being inside all day," I explained as I pulled him back.

Wanda Sue straightened. "That little poodle is just cuter than a June bug on a hot night."

I kept a tight hold on Kong's leash as he tried to nip at Wanda Sue's ankle. He didn't like being compared to insects, and I swear he could understand English—even with Wanda Sue's heavy southern accent and occasional mangling of the language. While I kept a wary eye on my poodle, I filled her in on the events that had transpired at the restaurant.

"If you ask me, Marco Santini deserved it," Wanda Sue commented when my narrative had ended.

I blinked in surprise. "Huh?"

She sniffed. "That man was mean as a snake—through and through. He drove his wife, Delores—Beatrice's mama—to a nervous breakdown just to hightail it away from him."

"How so?" My interest kindled.

"Anger issues." She pursed her lips. "But to tell you the honest truth, I think Delores faked the breakdown. Afterward, she moved into town and found herself a new man—some mystery guy—no one actually ever met him. Anyway, she was a happy camper until she got Lucas Disease."

I paused, trying to decipher her usage. "You mean lupus?"

"Yeah, that's it. Poor Delores—couldn't go in the sun for years, just like them werewolves. Eventually, she got weaker, and she died a couple of years ago. Tragic. I liked her. She was a sweet lady and deserved better than she got in life."

"And now Beatrice has lost both parents," I said, almost to myself. A twinge of guilt nagged at me for all the times that I complained about my own mother. Sure, she could be controlling, but at least I had both parents in good health—with a two-thousand-mile buffer. It couldn't get much better.

Her brows drawn together, Wanda Sue looked out over the Gulf of Mexico; the gently rolling waves seemed to sigh at the story of the Santini family. "At least Beatrice has Guido."

"Her boyfriend from the restaurant?"

"Yep." A small puff of breeze wafted in, and she tucked an imaginary stray hair up into the massive bouffant. Nothing had actually been blown free, because Wanda Sue probably used half a can of hair spray a day to keep that helmet firmly in place. "He came here six months ago as an exchange student from Sicily and worked in the restaurant part-time—just a dear boy. He and Beatrice were an item right from the beginning—like Rodeo and Juliet. So romantic." She let out a long, audible breath.

"Guido sounds like a good kid," I echoed. Obviously, Shakespeare hadn't been on Wanda Sue's required high school reading list.

"He is, but Marco never liked him—what a surprise. He did everything he could to keep them apart, 'cause he wanted Beatrice to take care of him in his old age, which wasn't all that far away." Wanda Sue clucked her tongue. "I told you, honey: mean as a snake."

"But Marco kept Guido working at Little Tuscany." I didn't want to tell her that I'd already heard part of this story from Sandy, because once Wanda Sue lost her train of thought, it never came back. "That's strange."

"Probably so he could keep an eye on him. It wasn't out of the goodness of his heart—trust me."

I did. Wanda Sue might not know the names of Shake-speare's star-crossed lovers, but she was a good judge of human nature. Maybe because she'd been managing the RV park for eons and had seen pretty much every kind of human behavior. I trusted her gut reaction more than the regularity of the sunrise and sunset.

We didn't speak for a few moments, with only the waves as a quiet background to our thoughts. The after-noon sun had intensified, and I plucked at my cotton T-shirt to cool off.

"Enjoy the heat, hon. A cold front is coming in off the Gulf." She pointed at the gray clouds off to the west.

"Wanda Sue, do you think it's a little odd that both Santini men died within two days of each other?" I finally asked.

"What do you mean?"

"Well . . . Carlos Santini died at home—of an appar-ent heart attack—and today Marco Santini died in his restaurant—of an apparent allergic reaction. Doesn't that strike you as sort of an . . . interesting coincidence?"

She wrinkled her nose and shook her head. "When you hit middle age, almost anything can snuff you out. Maude Butterman, who used to live here at the Twin Palms, caught one of those retroactive viruses and, in three days—poof! Gone. Of course, she'd had a couple of mini strokes beforehand, but—you never know." She hugged her arms across her ample chest. "She'd parked her RV for years right here on the spot next to yours."

I started. "You mean I'm next to a death-cootie RV site?"

"Oh, no," she reassured me. "The cooties are gone. I had Pop Pop clean the site after we had her RV hauled away."

Like that was going to help. Pop Pop probably had his own death cooties seeping out of every pore ever since he'd turned eighty. He could barely stand, much less hold a garden hose to clean off a cement pad. I made a vow to myself to throw a couple of gallon jugs of bleach over the RV site at the first chance. No death cootie could survive that.

"You know . . . I thought I saw an RV parked next to me," I said, "and it looked like an older version of my Airstream."

Wanda Sue waved her arm dismissively. "Oh, no, honey—that site isn't rented till November."

Odd. But it had been a long day. "So you don't think the brothers' deaths could be related or . . . suspicious?"

Wanda Sue's heavily made-up eyes gleamed in sudden curiosity. "Was Madame Geri with you today?"

"Uh-huh."

"What did *she* think?"

"Nothing specific." I averted my glance briefly, and then Kong scratched at my leg—that was his I've-desperately-got-to-pee signal. "Sorry, can't talk now. Kong needs to find a palmetto bush."

Wanda Sue blocked me by stretching out both arms. "I don't believe you. Something is up. Dish."

"All right." I sighed, keeping Kong reined in next to me; he tapped one little paw in irritation. I revved up my motormouth. "This morning, Madame Geri popped into the *Observer* office in a panic, saying that a killer was loose on the island who could cause a problem with Jimmy and Sandy's wedding. That was right after I started investigating Carlos Santini's death, which seemed a little suspicious to me; after that, we went to Little Tuscany to question his brother about Carlos' demise, and . . . well, you know, he died from some kind of allergy—"

"Oh no." Wanda Sue crossed herself. "If you can't figure out what happened to the two brothers, something about their deaths will link back to poor ol' Jimmy—I just know it. And then he'll end up in jail, and Sandy might meet someone else while he's locked away—"

"Whoa. Time out." I made the letter *T* with my hands. "You're getting *way* ahead of yourself. We don't even know if there was anything fishy about Carlos' or Marco's deaths."

"Lordy, girl, don't you get it? If Madame Geri thinks the wedding could be off on account of the island killer, it's off." She touched my arm. "Unless *you* can figure out a way to make sure it's back on."

"For goodness' sake, don't repeat the 'killer' part; it'll panic every islander with a pulse—and then some." Tilting back my head for a few moments, I tried to block out the image of my aging neighbors in a tizzy with their walkers and oxygen tanks. This being-part-of-a-community thing had its drawbacks: like I had to get involved in stuff that didn't or shouldn't concern me.

"Please, Mallie, you have to help."

I paused. "All right. I'll give it my best shot," I finally said in a reluctant tone.

Wanda Sue clapped her hands. "I knew we could count on you, honey."

"This could all be Madame Geri's bunk—"

"Then you can help Sandy finish up her wedding plans," she responded with a huge smile. "You're just a regular Emily Post-it."

High praise. Just call me the Queen of "sticky etiquette."

"I'll get Pop Pop to tidy up the RV site next to you in two shakes—just in case any death cooties are still hanging around." Wanda Sue jaunted off after giving me a big hug and an air kiss.

The only thing that would be "shaking" on Pop Pop was his arthritic hands, but I guessed it was worth a try if I left him the bleach in full sight.

"Come on, Kong, I've got to get ready for my dates." I looked down at him, feeling my excitement build at hearing myself utter the word *dates*. *Oh boy.* "Stress the plural—I've got *two* dinner dates. Can you believe it?"

He cocked his head to one side, as if to say, "Fat chance."

"It's true, and I'm going to enjoy every minute of the evening."

Kong lifted his leg and peed on my Birkenstock. Not an auspicious sign.

An hour later, after an invigorating shower and some serious primping in my bedroom, I'd forgotten the peeing incident, having washed off my sandals, and I tried to forget what had happened at Little Tuscany— and Madame Geri's ominous warning about the wedding.

This was "double date" night, which I was hoping would help to banish the memory of Marco's death— and all the talk about an island killer afoot.

Taking stock of myself in the mirror gave me the good and bad news. The good: thick, curly red hair and a slim figure; the bad: freckles everywhere (even in my ears) and a flat chest. But with a little tinted moisturizer, mascara, and pink lipstick, I did the most with my girl-next-door looks.

I peered closer at the massive splattering of freckles on my face—*nothing* except cement would cover them.

Then again, maybe I should slather on some of that bee cream. I'd tried everything else to fade the freckles—

A knock on my Airstream door interrupted my fantasy of a smooth, freckle-free face.

Kong looked up at me and didn't bark—that meant he knew the knock.

Cole.

I took my time, strolling through the Airstream, taking in deep breaths, and chanting my Tae Kwon Do mantra, *muggatoni,* to steady my nerves.

It didn't work.

I'd finally reached the dating zenith after a long, long drought. Double fun by having two guys, two restaurants, and two dinners. Who could keep calm at that prospect?

Then, I swung open the door with a beaming grin and beheld Cole . . . and Nick Billie.

My heart sank.

The smile faded.

There stood my blond, surfer-dude boyfriend in casual shorts and a T-shirt holding a spray of wildflowers; and my dark-haired potential boyfriend in dress pants and jacket, clutching a large box of chocolates—staring at me with eyes filled with confusion . . . and hurt. *Oh no.*

Could two men appear in greater contrast to each other? Except now they both wore similar grim expressions.

"Hi." *What else could I say?*

Heat rose to my face, and it had nothing to do with the temperature. *Busted.*

"I guess I'm late," Cole said, his voice flat.

"I guess I'm early," Nick said, his voice strained.

"I . . . uh, guess I have some explaining to do," I stammered.

Both men waited in mute anticipation.

My mouth opened and closed a few times, but nothing came out.

Don't fail me now, motormouth.

"Okay, I know this looks bad, but it really makes sense, considering what happened today. Anita just assigned me to be the new food critic for the *Observer* this morning, and I have to go to two different restaurants tonight—and then write blog reviews for both of them. But I didn't want to eat alone, and I didn't want to have to . . . well, burden one of you with going to two restaurants in one night." I turned to Nick. "And then when you pulled me over for nearly running down that old guy on the three-wheeler—"

"You almost ran over an elderly biker?" Cole cut in.

"He turned in front of me. It wasn't my fault." I swung my glance in Cole's direction, happy that at least my motormouth had seemed to kick into gear during my time of need. "But then Nick mentioned dinner, so I suggested Pelican's Grill, knowing I couldn't cancel Le Sink—"

"You mean you were going to have dinner at the nice restaurant with *him* after taking *me* to that dumpy place with all the sinks in the front yard?" The hurt in Cole's soft blue eyes deepened.

Okay, it was official. This wasn't going well.

"Cole, it's not like that. It's just that you and I had already planned on something casual, and I couldn't cancel on you just because Anita wanted another food review tonight." Mentally kicking myself, I plunged onward. "I know you don't like to wear a suit—"

"That's not the point. I thought we were a couple." He tossed the wildflowers to the ground. "I would've bought a suit, if it meant that much to you."

Definitely not going well. Even beyond that, I felt like a consummate weasel.

I turned back to my potential island-cop boyfriend (though now that seemed a remote possibility).

"Nick, I didn't want to turn down your invitation since you were so kind to ask—and Anita wanted me to do a review of Pelican's Grill." I swallowed as if a boulder blocked my throat. Who had I been kidding? I wasn't the type of girl who could handle dating one guy, much less two.

He lifted one dark eyebrow, handed me the box of chocolates, and left without a word.

Cole followed and retreated into his van.

I stood there, chocolates in hand and wildflowers at my feet, with no one to blame but myself. Kong nuzzled my ankle, picking up on my dejection, but this once, my pooch's affection couldn't remedy my downcast mood.

I felt like a wrung-out dishrag. How could I have been so stupid?

Just then, Pop Pop zoomed up in his golf cart, taking

out a bougainvillea bush before he could apply the brakes.

"Hiya, Mallie."

I tried to summon a smile but managed only a slight twist of my lips.

"Wanda Sue said you needed the site next to you cleaned." He slowly heaved his skinny legs out from behind the wheel and grabbed his cane and a bottle of Windex. Of course, he couldn't juggle both at the same time, and I had to rush up and grab the Windex.

"Be careful." I rubbed my forehead in frustration. "I think she wanted you to use Tilex."

"Darn it, I thought Wanda Sue said *Windex*." His wrinkles deepened as he looked at the bottle in puzzlement; then he tapped his left ear. "My hearing aid batteries must be running low again."

"Maybe so." I raised my voice and enunciated each word with exaggerated deliberateness.

"I guess since I'm here, I could clean the front windows on your Airstream—"

"No need." I grabbed the Windex bottle from him and tossed it into the back of his golf cart. The last thing I wanted was for Pop Pop to stand on a ladder balancing his cane and a bottle of Windex on those shaky, skinny legs, trying to clean my large Airstream windows.

A recipe for a broken hip if I'd ever heard one.

"Okay, if you insist." I could hear the relief in his voice.

He leaned forward, both hands on his cane. "You look mighty nice, Miss Mallie."

"Thanks, Pop Pop." I set the chocolates on my picnic table with a sigh.

He looked over at Cole's buttoned-up van. "Did your boyfriend back out on the date?"

"Sort of." No point in trying to explain—Pop Pop wouldn't hear me anyway. I picked up the wildflowers and set them next to the chocolates. "And I was going to write a review of the restaurant where we were having dinner, so I guess I'll be eating alone."

"A pretty girl like you? Nah." He shook his head, but the motion seemed to loosen his dentures, and he had to shift his jaw to move them back into place. "I'd be proud to go with you."

Huh?

"I know it's not a real date or anything, 'cause I'm a little old for you, but we could share dinner."

Little old? He was ancient, almost a mummy.

Still, the hopeful kindness in his sagging face tugged at my heart. "I don't know if your offer will stand if you hear where I have to eat—Le Sink."

"I *love* it there," he enthused, which led to a cackle, which led to a cough and my slapping him on the back so he could catch his breath.

He finally straightened.

"Okay—it's a date," I said, realizing Madame Geri had been right. This was my karma for being deceitful: sharing dinner with a geriatric RV park handyman with bad dentures. It couldn't get much worse.

"You'll have to drive, Mallie, and I'll need to pick up

my medication on the way there," he pronounced. "If I don't take my pills, dinner goes right through me, and I can't even make it home in time."

Okay, it just got worse.

Twenty minutes later, I had loaded Pop Pop, his newly purchased pills, his cane, and his oxygen tank (just in case) into my truck, and we headed out to Le Sink.

Luckily, Rusty's air conditioner had kicked in, and we had a few puffs of coolness coming from the vents. Pop Pop took ten minutes to fasten his seat belt and then leaned his head back on the headrest to recover from his efforts. At least I had a few minutes of quiet as I drove to Le Sink.

This was turning out to be one heck of day: Madame Geri's ominous predictions about an island killer, watching a man die, and then hurting the two men in my life.

When would I finally get my act together?

Pop Pop coughed a few more times, and my attention swung back to my date. "Are you okay?"

"Yeah . . . just some phlegm." He cleared his throat, opened the window, and spit.

I just kept my eyes on the road, almost clapping when I saw the sign for Le Sink.

"Here we are!" I turned into the parking lot, and Rusty lurched over the potholes into a spot near a Porta Potti, which I assumed served as the public toilet for the restaurant—as per Sandy's warning.

I vowed not to drink any liquids.

We climbed out of the truck and ambled toward the

open-air restaurant that appeared just like the image on the Web site: a trailer with a serving window, a dozen or so paint-chipped picnic tables, and ceramic sinks littered around as yard ornaments.

A middle-aged couple sat at one of the tables; they both wore that resigned, desperate look of people who'd long given up ever expecting any food—or service, for that matter.

As we headed for a table, I realized that, in fact, the Web site didn't quite do it justice. The picnic tables had a layer of grime not apparent in the picture, and the sinks seemed to emanate a moldy smell that couldn't quite be captured in a visual image.

Charming.

I settled Pop Pop at one of the tables and signaled the waitress to come over. She looked at us and commented to the guy at the grill, "Crap . . . more customers."

Grabbing a couple of paper menus, she sauntered over and slapped them onto our table. "You want some water?" she asked in a bored tone.

"I'd like an iced tea," Pop Pop said.

"All we have is water," she answered, a hand on her hip; the other hand shoved back her stringy Goth-black hair.

"Sounds good to me." Pop Pop smiled but received no reaction in response.

I glanced over at the Porta Potti briefly. "Nothing for me, thanks." I sneaked my notepad out of my hobo bag, ready to start taking notes for my review.

As she stomped off, the middle-aged couple waved their arms overhead for attention like a ground crew trying to land an aircraft. She ignored them, and the man shouted: "We still don't have our burgers, and it's been almost two hours!"

"Order up," the cook said from the trailer grill. She grabbed the plastic baskets containing burgers and fries and took them over to the couple. The man stared down at his meal and then looked up in disbelief.

"This is burned to a crisp," he said, nudging it as if it were contagious.

"You said you wanted yours well done," she said. "So?"

"Mine is raw; I asked for medium," the woman with him complained.

The waitress muttered something under her breath, turned her back on them, and strode back to our table. "What do you want?"

I scanned the menu. Two items were typed on the paper: *Burger* and *Cheeseburger.* "I guess I'll have the cheeseburger—medium well." I figured that I might luck out and get something in between raw and burned.

"I'll have a fish sandwich." Of course, Pop Pop couldn't read the menu.

"You'll have the burger," our waitress said, ordering for him, and left.

Pop Pop turned to me with a smile. "Isn't this place great? I'd come here every week if I could get Wanda Sue to give me more time off."

"But you don't drive," I pointed out, not to mention that

his job at the Twin Palms wasn't exactly twenty-four/ seven—if you didn't count his nap time. Still, you couldn't fault his upbeat attitude—even on the threshold of dining hell.

"Wanda Sue drops me off," he explained, moving around his dentures with his tongue. "She always says she'd rather be hog-tied than eat here."

At that moment, the waitress returned with a glass of water; the liquid looked yellowish. *Ick.*

"Okay, enough!" I stood up, marched past the waitress, and poked my head inside the trailer's serving counter. "Hey, you!"

A young guy, with a grease-encrusted spatula in hand, looked up from the grill. "What?"

"My friend's water is yel-*low*," I stated, emphasizing the last syllable.

"It's well water." He slapped a mound of hamburger onto the grill; it flared in a mini cloud of grease and smoke.

"It's *dirty* water."

"Says you." He shrugged and slapped another mound of hamburger onto the grill, which sizzled in an even larger sooty cloud.

"Look, just so you know, I'm Mallie Monroe from the *Observer,* and I'm doing a review of your . . . uh, restaurant for the paper's blog." I rapped my hand on the counter. "And you're not earning too many stars by treating my dining companion like he's some kind of pathetic old derelict."

I gestured at Pop Pop, who had removed his dentures and dropped them into the glass of water.

"Looks like he found a use for the water," Grill Guy commented as he focused on charring our burgers.

"A bad review could close you down," I warned.

"Good luck!" The middle-aged couple both gave me a thumbs-up.

"Fat chance," Grill Guy muttered.

"Fine," I said. "We'll eat that garbage you're cooking, and I'll make certain everyone on the island knows—"

"Kyle!" a man shouted from behind me.

Grill Guy halted and peered out the counter opening. "Guido, what the hell are you doing here? I thought I told you not to come back here—"

"Silenzio!" Guido threw open the trailer door, shouting words in Italian.

Kyle the Grill Guy appeared at the door with the spatula, and Guido lunged at him hollering:

"Killer! You killed Mr. Santini!"

Chapter Four

The two young men tussled for a few minutes as Guido aimed several weak punches at Kyle's face. Kyle slapped Guido repeatedly with the plastic spatula. Neither of them would exactly qualify for a heavyweight title. Or even a lightweight one.

"Killer!" Guido shouted as he yanked Kyle out of the trailer.

Kyle stumbled but never let go of the spatula. "You're crazy." He thumped his assailant on the ear with his plastic weapon.

Guido torpedoed into Kyle, grabbing him around the waist and wrestling him to the ground. "I am not! *Bastardo!* You will pay for what you did to Mr. Santini and Beatrice."

They rolled around on the sand and gravel, grunting and pummeling each other.

I stood there, transfixed—not sure if I should call the police or get Guido his own spatula. Then they rolled in my direction, and I jumped back.

"Stop it!" I clapped my hands to get their attention.

Neither responded. Kyle grabbed a fistful of sand and threw it into Guido's face. He spat it out and grabbed some broken shells, which he rubbed into Kyle's stringy hair. They stuck in the black strands, causing a salt-and-pepper effect.

"Hey, can someone assist me here?" I turned to the waitress.

"Not my problem." She strolled past me with two small food baskets in hand. I caught a whiff of charred burger and almost gagged. But Pop Pop retrieved his teeth from the glass, snapped them into place, and smiled eagerly as the bored Goth girl served him.

"Thank you kindly, miss," he said, picking up a French fry. "Yum."

"Damn it," said Kyle, trying to shake the shells out of his hair as he kept up the spatula attack. "Let go of me."

"Never!" said Guido, jerking his head from side to side to avoid the blows.

"Help!" I appealed to no one in particular.

"Whaddya say?" Pop Pop tapped his hearing aid.

"The guys are fighting over here, and they won't stop." I pointed down at the rolling, scuffling duo.

Pop Pop sprang into action: he grabbed the edge of the picnic table and inched to an upright stance, peering over at the trailer. When he realized what was going on, he thumped his hand on the tabletop. "Cut that out, youngsters!"

His burger basket flipped upward, and the meat patty fell to the ground.

"Oh no." His face fell in disappointment.

"You can have *my* burger, Pop Pop . . . I need some assistance here." I tried to catch Guido's shirt, but they rolled in the other direction right at the moment I had almost grasped the collar.

"I'll get my oxygen tank," he suggested, making for the truck with the speed of a turtle. "One whiff, and I can take on both of them."

Huh? I looked around in desperation. If this fight didn't stop, they were going to end up hurting each other—by accident. *I've got to do something.* I scanned the outside part of the trailer and saw nothing but an old wooden broom. I paused, weighing its possible effect versus Pop Pop's potential oxygen-tank rejuvenation. Then I spied Kyle reaching for a large rock as the guys rolled in the direction of a palm tree. Instantly, I snatched the broom and began to rap Guido and Kyle on their backs.

"Enough already!" I whacked them a couple more times, inadvertently hitting Guido in the face. He gave a little yelp and let go of Kyle, who scrambled away from him, dropping the rock and shaking the sand out of his hair.

"What's the hell is the matter with you, dude?" Kyle exclaimed as he drew in a ragged breath.

Panting, Guido wiped the sweat from his brow. "I know what you did. Mr. Santini is dead, and you killed him."

"You're crazy." Kyle picked sand out of his ear.

"I should've jammed it down your throat."

Kyle glared at him. "Just try it."

"Take it easy." I clutched the broom, ready to strike if the boys started up again.

"I'm coming." Pop Pop wheeled his oxygen tank in between the two boys, cranking it on and taking a deep whiff.

Guido's dark eyes widened, taking in the menacing Pop Pop persona with his shriveled body hidden in a loose-fitting sports shirt, knee-length plaid shorts, and orthopedic wingtips.

Scary, all right.

Pop Pop straightened his skinny shoulders and shook a bony finger in Guido's direction. "Now you've gotta deal with me, and I don't take any guff, let me tell you." He turned to Kyle. "And not from you either."

Kyle muttered something under his breath, his body still tense and ready for another attack from Guido.

Pop Pop then started coughing and doubled over, dropping his oxygen mask on the ground. The two guys immediately rushed to his aid, grabbing his arms and holding him upright. I tried to take control of the oxygen-tank equipment, as I fumbled with the mask. Eventually, I managed to get it over his face.

"Take a few deep breaths," I said, as I patted him on the shoulder.

He complied, but one side of his mouth turned upward, and he gave me wink, whispering, "Geezer power."

My mouth dropped open. He'd been faking the whole coughing fit to distract them.

Aging Machiavellian tactics. Cool. I was lost in admiration of Pop Pop's craftiness—and his acting skills. Maybe there was something to that whole "not getting older but better" thing.

"Let's get him into the truck," I said, trying to sound very concerned over Pop Pop's state of health. That probably worked better than the old broom at defusing the situation.

"Don't forget my burger," he added in a weak voice. "And the fries . . ."

"Sure thing." It was the least I could do, even if it would give my truck a funky smell. I retrieved the basket with the crisped burger, paid the Goth waitress, who had retreated inside the trailer to put on another layer of black eyeliner, and reached my truck just at the point Guido was strapping the seat belt around Pop Pop.

Kyle opened the back door and set the oxygen tank on the floor. He stepped away as I approached.

"Look, thanks for helping with Pop Pop," I began, handing the hockey-puck hamburger patty to my aging handyman. He eagerly gobbled down half of it before I could slam the door shut. Shuddering, I turned to the two guys. "You know I can't just forget what happened here—one of you could've really been hurt—so I'm going to have to file a report with Detective Billie tomorrow. In the meantime, Guido, hop into the back, and I'll take you home."

"What about my bicycle?"

"Throw it into the back of the truck."

"Okay." A shadow of fear touched Guido's face. "Will I get in trouble for fighting with Kyle? I don't want to be sent back to Italia and leave my darling Beatrice— 'specially not now. She's all alone."

I hesitated, chewing on my lower lip.

"Please, miss," he pleaded.

"Let's talk about it—I might be persuaded to put in a good word for you." Of course, I didn't add that my stock with Nick Billie had tanked lower than a Florida sink-hole.

He placed the bike in the back of Rusty and then climbed in. Kyle ambled back to the trailer, looking over his shoulder a couple of times. Then he aimed a rude hand gesture at Guido, who, luckily, didn't notice.

"Jerk," I mumbled, as I circled around the front of Rusty. Kyle might not be a killer, but he certainly needed a first-class attitude adjustment—and a grill that didn't look like an outpost on the verge of Milton's city of Pandemonium in *Paradise Lost.*

I cranked up Rusty's engine and pulled out of the parking lot with my motley crew. After a few moments of inhaling the hideous stench of the burger, I rolled down my window. Of course, halfway down, it stuck. I gasped for some fresh air and then reconciled myself to possible asphyxiation.

As I turned onto Cypress Drive, the island's main drag, I noticed the sun had begun to set. Various shades of red streaked across the sky like blotches of anger and dark menace.

Blood and fire.

I shuddered inwardly. *What did it mean?*

Had Marco Santini been murdered? What about his brother? I didn't believe in coincidences, so my suspicions had been placed on high alert.

I glanced at Guido in the backseat. Had he been on to something when he accused Kyle?

"Want a bite?" Pop Pop shoved the burger into my face. I swallowed hard.

"Maybe a little one." I took the charred lump from him and nibbled the tiniest piece I could manage.

I blinked. It wasn't half-bad. Instead of tasting like charcoal, it had an appetizing, smoky flavor, much like you'd get at one of those expensive restaurants where they cook on a plank. I sneaked another bite—bigger this time—and savored the crunchy zing of Le Sink's main menu item.

"Told ya." Pop Pop retrieved the remaining burger from me and gobbled it down before I could come up with another excuse to get an additional bite.

Sighing, I contented myself by grabbing a few of his fries—and found those just as tasty. Crisp and lightly salted. *Yum.* Well, at least I'd have some positive aspects for my restaurant review. Le Sink might look like Le Dump and employ waitstaff who were Le Stupid,

but they served a lean and mean burger. I'd be back—
and without Pop Pop as my date. Then, I remembered
what had happened with my two erstwhile boyfriends
and sighed again.

I'd probably be dining alone.

"Miss, can I explain what happened?" Guido asked
in a tentative voice.

"Sure." I helped myself to a few more fries, thinking
Pop Pop wouldn't see me. He moved the basket out of
my reach. *Damn.* "First, tell me where you live."

"At the island center—behind the Circle K."

"Okay, so what's your story, Guido? Why did you attack Kyle?" I glanced at his worried young face, shadowed dark eyes, and tight-lipped mouth. The picture of
anxiety.

"I saw Kyle in the Little Tuscany kitchen this morning.
He used to work for Mr. Santini in the restaurant, but he
doesn't anymore. So he had no business being there."
Guido shook his head. "Then Mr. Santini died, and no
one knows why."

My interest perked. "Why did Kyle leave his job at
the restaurant?"

"Mr. Santini fired him."

The perk had started to simmer. "Really? Why?"

"I think he was caught stealing money from the cash
register, but I don't know for sure."

"So Kyle might be a thief, but that doesn't mean he's
a killer," I pointed out, the perk reaching a boiling point
of curiosity.

"He also said mean things to Beatrice." Guido's mouth thinned in anger. "No one talks bad to my *bella* Beatrice—not even her father. He wasn't always nice to his own daughter."

"Young love . . . isn't it wonderful?" Pop Pop commented with a benign smile.

"Lovely," I echoed, checking on Guido again. A flicker of rage passed across his features, but then he got control of himself and resumed his normal nice-guy persona. Could *he* have done something bad to Carlos to protect Beatrice? He was obviously head-over-heels, smitten-to-the-core in love with the girl. And, if she had been upset over her father's treatment, maybe Guido had decided to take matters into his own hands and eliminate the problem.

Was it possible?

I gave myself a mental shake, realizing that the events of the day must have skewed all my common sense. Guido was nothing more than a guy in love who'd seen his girl collapse in grief as her father died in front of her eyes. That's all. And that was enough.

I couldn't take much more myself. The last twenty-four hours had included a dire prophecy, an agonizing death, and dashed dreams of actually having two men vie for my affections. Not to mention that I'd reached a new low of having a rebound dinner date with a man on oxygen.

I needed my Airstream, my teacup poodle, and a good night's sleep. Things would look better tomorrow in the a.m.

"Oops. My dentures just fell out," Pop Pop pronounced.

Great.

The morning seemed a long way off.

It had turned dark by the time we dropped off Guido and made our way back to the Twin Palms RV park. When we arrived, I had to get a flashlight to locate Pop Pop's missing false teeth, which had rolled under the seat. *Yuck.*

Ready to tear out my curls, I finally deposited him, his dentures, and his oxygen tank at his cottage and revved off to my Airstream.

Needless to say, it wasn't exactly the end I'd imagined to my big date night. My spirits sank lower than a gator in the mud, to quote Wanda Sue. And it was nothing more than I deserved for trying to be a dating diva.

Sigh. I parked in front of my Airstream and took in the blue-and-white striped awning flapping in the light evening breeze coming off the Gulf.

Ah. Home, sweet home.

I could hear Kong barking in excitement as I turned off my engine, and despite my fatigue, a little glow lit inside me. At least my dog still provided unconditional love, constant attention, and ankle licking whenever I needed a boost. As I unlocked the door, Kong came bounding out, and I scooped him up in my arms. I allowed myself to revel in his adoration for a few moments before I grabbed his leash and made for the surf.

After a long stroll along the beach, I headed back to my Airstream, its shiny hull bathed in the moonlight.

Cole's van remained parked on one side, though his bicycle was gone, so I assumed he was riding in the dark, trying to forget my two-timing behavior. Couldn't say that I blamed him.

My glance trailed to the other side of my RV, and, just as had happened earlier today, I thought I saw the outline of another Airstream. A light glowed from the inside, but the shades were drawn.

I squinted in the dim light, trying to focus my eyes more clearly. Then I blinked, and it was gone.

Strange.

I gave myself a mental shake. Somehow it must have been a reflection of my own Airstream, but . . . not exactly a twin image.

"I'm either losing it," I said to Kong, "or I need glasses."

He barked.

"Okay—maybe both." I hurried him along, taking one last longing glace at Cole's van before Kong and I retreated inside. I fixed myself a bowl of soup, gave my poodle a gourmet doggy treat, and powered up my laptop to work on my restaurant review of Le Sink while I ate my dinner-for-one (person, that is).

Needless to say, my evaluation was mixed: a one-trick menu, surly waitstaff, and ghettolike ambiance. But I had to admit, the burger tasted scrumptious—thick, juicy, and smoky-flavored—and the French fries were crisp and salty. I gave it two out of five stars—one star deducted because of having to break up the fistfight with a broom.

Thinking about that part of the evening made me sit back in my chair and reflect on the events of the day. My mouth also began to water, remembering the brief taste of Pop Pop's burger in my truck. Instantly, I dumped the soup in the garbage and heated up some leftover pizza— served with a side of potato chips.

That's more like it.

As I munched the thick cheese and pepperoni, I tried to get back into the Le Sink review, but I couldn't. I stared at my computer screen, but the image of Marco's death, Beatrice's reaction, Guido's fight—and Pop Pop's dentures—kept reverberating through my mind. They all *had* to be connected (except the false teeth), but I didn't know how.

And how did these events relate to Carlos Santini's death a few days ago? Two brothers within a week? It just couldn't be a coincidence.

"What do you think, Kong?" I asked my canine companion, but he had curled up on my sofa and fallen asleep.

I mulled over the events one more time, but nothing occurred to me. *Maybe Madame Geri knows.*

Okay, now I knew it was time to pack it in and get some rest, but first, I had to finish the review.

Once I knocked it out, I scooped up Kong and headed to the bedroom part of my Airstream, feeling a sudden chill.

Was it all this contemplation of death? I shivered again and then slid into bed and flipped on the TV.

A perky blond weathergirl in a low-cut top and tight skirt appeared, pointing at a map of Florida. "A cold front is dipping down into southwest Florida, and the temperature might drop thirty degrees overnight," she said, smiling into the camera with a flash of even white teeth. "Time to get out the sweaters and scarves."

I flipped my thermostat to HEAT and cranked up the dial.

Nothing happened.

The Florida winter had begun early, and my heater was on the blink.

Yikes.

By the time morning arrived, I awoke under my heavy layer of quilts, aware that Kong had snuggled under the blankets with me—and that the temperature inside my Airstream had taken on a distinct chill.

Reluctantly, I slid out of bed, easing Kong onto the floor and wrapping the quilt around me for warmth. I picked up my cell phone and dialed Sam—the island's handyman. If there was one person who could figure out how to get my heater working, it was Sam.

My fingers drummed against the cell phone with impatience as I waited for Sam to pick up. But he didn't. I got his voice mail instead.

"Sam, my heater is broken, and I'm desperate. I can't call Pop Pop to help out because we had a date last night at Le Sink, then there was a big fight, and I ended up taking Guido home, and Pop Pop later lost his dentures in my truck." Okay, despite the cold, my motormouth hadn't officially chilled out. "Anyway, I'm freezing my patootie off in the Airstream."

I clicked the cell phone shut, debating whether or not I could manage a shower without getting hypothermia. Then I heard a knock at my door.

I swung it open and beheld Pop Pop, wearing a blue flannel shirt, baggy sweatpants, and gloves. He looked like a scarecrow. "I thought you might need this, since the cold front came through, and I know your Airstream is kind of old."

Holding up a space heater in one hand, he managed to balance the oxygen tank and a bouquet of flowers in the other.

I grinned at the sight of the heater and seized it as if it were a lifeline.

"I have to take care of you now that we're dating." He held out the flowers.

The grin faded. *Huh?*

"We most definitely are *not* a couple, but I will take the heater." I closed the door on him quickly. That's all I needed: a geriatric suitor to fill in the gap left by the hasty departures of Cole and Nick last night. I wasn't that desperate. Besides, they'd be back—or so I hoped.

I peeped out my window and saw Pop Pop rev off in his golf cart. My glance slid over to Cole's van—still no sign of him.

Regretful, I turned away from the window, heater in

hand. At least Pop Pop had left before anyone had seen him at my door with flowers.

I headed for the shower.

An hour later, I strolled into the *Observer* office. Sandy greeted me from her desk, ensconced in a brown and yellow knit poncho. Anita stood next to her, sporting a pea green velour warm-up suit. Needless to say, my own outfit of jeans and moth-eaten sweater wasn't exactly an ensemble out of *Vogue*. But it so rarely turned this frigid in Florida, people tended not to invest in cold-weather gear—including me.

"That temperature drop last night caught me off guard," I commented, sitting at my desk and flipping on the computer. "Brr."

I rubbed my hands together for emphasis.

Sandy giggled.

"What's up?" I swiveled my chair around. "I thought you'd be a basket case after Madame Geri's prediction and the events at Little Tuscany yesterday."

"That's before we heard you were dating Pop Pop," Anita responded with a wry nod. "You're hitting the bottom of the barrel, kiddo."

My mouth thinned. "I am *not* dating Pop Pop!"

"But we heard that you had dinner with him last night at Le Sink," Sandy said in an amused voice. "That must've been fun—"

"Oh, for goodness' sake, it wasn't like a date—the

man has to be a hundred and fifty if he's a day," I protested. "The only reason I went with him is I got busted
trying to go out with Cole and Nick Billie on the same
night—"

"What?" Sandy's brown eyes widened into saucers.
"Nick and Cole together? Yow. Did they have a fistfight?
I'll bet Nick Billie could kick butt."

"No, they didn't get physical. When they saw each
other, they both just left—with me holding flowers and
chocolates but no guy."

"Chocolates?" Sandy's tone turned wistful. "Godiva?"
I nodded.

"My favorite." She smacked her lips. "The dark kind?
Or the—"

"Okay, enough of this crap," Anita cut in, sitting on the
corner of Sandy's desk. "And for the record, if you want
to date a guy who hasn't chewed his own food since the
disco era, I could care less. But I do care that you did
your restaurant review."

I produced my flash drive with a flourish. "Finished it
this morning." Placing it in her outstretched palm, I
continued, "Also for the record, Pop Pop has a nice set
of dentures."

Her fingers closed around the small drive. "Spoken
like a woman in love."

I leveled a mean glare in her direction and headed for
the Mr. Coffee.

She cackled. "Did you include anything about Marco's
death? That would make a tasty little dessert—"

"Wait a minute." I stopped mid-pour. "I reviewed Le Sink—and skipped Little Tuscany because Marco died. I was going to drop by Pelican's Grill today—"

"Jeez Louise. Do I have to explain everything?" She tossed the drive onto my desk, as I strolled back with my steaming cup of java. "Post the Le Sink review, skip the stop at Pelican's Grill, and add a blog update of Little Tuscany, complete with the owner's death right in the middle of your meal. That's what sells papers—not some sappy garbage about crisp salads and creamy sauces. Spare me."

"But I didn't have time to take more than two bites of my pasta at Little Tuscany before Marco staggered out of the kitchen—"

"That's plenty of sampling for the review. The food is only the entrée to the main course: Marco expiring in his own dining room."

Sandy and I turned silent.

"Get it? The entrée?"

"Uh-huh." I took a deep swig of coffee.

Anita gave an exclamation of disgust, mumbling how no one in the office "got" her wit. "Write up the review, kiddo, and have it on my desk by the end of the day."

"All right." I flipped on my desktop PC; it made audible beeps as it slowly fired up. "Um . . . is Nick investigating Marco's death?"

"Trying to get back in Billie's good graces?" Anita lifted one eyebrow.

"No." Well, that wasn't exactly true. "I wanted to tell

him about what went down at Le Sink last night. Guido got into a wrestling match with Kyle the Grill Guy—"

"Over the bad food?" Sandy inquired.

"Not exactly. Guido called Kyle a murderer and then just attacked him. They tumbled and thumped each other on the ground till I separated them with an old broom."

Sandy's face kindled with interest—and a touch of puzzlement. "So Marco's death might be suspicious?"

"Possibly." I recalled the restaurateur's final moments, red-faced, choking, and clawing at the air. I shivered. "Now, whether or not Kyle was responsible for his death is another thing. I don't see the connection—"

"Kyle's mother, Francesca, owns Taste of Venice—Marco's biggest competition." Anita yawned. "Personally, I hate all Italian food, but I guess their rivalry was legendary. Rumor has it, Francesca stole one of Marco's prized recipes and won some national recipe contest, and he was going to sue her. That might be motive."

"And Marco hated her ever since?"

"Bingo."

I sat back in my chair, mulling over this revelation as I drained my cup. "What about Kyle? Is he close to his mother?"

Anita crossed her index and middle finger. "Like two peas in a pod."

"So he might've done in Marco for . . . his mother?" Something about that scenario just didn't ring true. I couldn't see Mr. Grill Guy actually taking the initiative to buy a gallon of milk, much less plan a murder.

"Stranger things have happened," Anita commented.

"I guess." I inserted my flash drive into the computer. The screen flickered and then went blank. I tapped the keys a few times, and it came to life again, except now a black line stretched across the screen. "Anita, I think this refurbished Dell is going down again."

"Maybe Santa will come early and bring you a new one—along with a lifetime supply of Poligrip for your new love."

Sandy giggled again.

"Not funny!" I turned on Sandy. "And you should know better. If someone killed Marco, your fiancé, Jimmy, might be a suspect."

Sandy's face crumpled, and tears sprang into her eyes. Instantly, I regretted my words.

"My poor Jimmy," she said, her head drooping. "Madame Geri was right—murder is afoot on the island, and my wedding will never take place. We're doomed."

"I'm sorry, Sandy." I reached across my desk and patted her hand. "That was stupid of me to say—your wedding will occur just the way you've planned it." I added a smile to reinforce my encouraging words.

"I've got to call Madame Geri," she said, picking up the phone and punching in some numbers.

I groaned.

"See what you did?" Anita gestured an imaginary gun in my direction. "Instead of riling up Sandy, you should be working on your review. If we don't sell papers, you don't have a job."

Didn't I know that? I'd had a string of low-level, low-income jobs as I had worked my way south from the Midwest, and the last thing I wanted was to lose my employment at the paper. Not that the island weekly comprised more than a few local stories, real estate ads, and Chamber of Commerce stuff, but I had a regular paycheck.

What could you do with a degree in comparative literature but hope and pray you didn't have to become a janitor to pay the rent?

Truth be told, I'd done even that: during my undistinguished tenure at Disney World, one of my jobs had been to walk around with one of those "trash grabbers" and clean up after the hordes of tourists who dropped everything from half-eaten turkey legs to used diapers—at seven bucks an hour.

"I'll have that review done in a jiffy," I said to Anita, poising my fingers above the keyboard.

"That's the attitude I want to hear." She hopped off Sandy's desk and tossed something at me. I caught it and looked down.

A jar of bee cream.

"You might slather some on Pop Pop and see if it helps with his those crevasselike wrinkles on his face." She cackled again. "See what it's done for me already?"

She patted her cheeks, which had taken on a bright red tint.

"It looks like an allergic reaction," I pointed out.

"Bull." She produced another jar, scooped out a large amount, and dabbed it around her eyes. "I'm getting the glow of beautiful skin."

I shrugged and turned back to my review of Little Tuscany. *Glow, my eye.* Let her face ignite into flames—as long as she didn't fire me.

I laughed inwardly at my own pun.

Anita strolled toward her tiny office. "When you're done, check with Nick about Marco's cause of death. We can always hope . . ."

"That he died of natural causes?" I finished for her.

"That someone killed him," she corrected me as she disappeared into her office.

Hag.

While Sandy chatted with Madame Geri on the phone, I grabbed another cup of coffee and knocked out the draft of my restaurant review for Little Tuscany. I covered the faux Italian décor, the mouthwatering pasta dishes, the homemade bread, and the owner's death throes—all within the 750-word count. It was my first foray into being an Official Food Critic, and I felt pleased with myself— even though I knew the small paragraph on Marco's tragic demise wouldn't be enough to please Anita.

After I saved the review on my flash drive, I printed out a hard copy and left it on Anita's desk while she was at lunch.

"I'm heading over to the island police station to check with Nick to see if he has any info about Marco's death," I told Sandy, as I picked up my hobo bag.

She placed her hand over the receiver's mouthpiece. "Madame Geri says Carlos' and Marco's deaths are related; the spirit world is sending her messages even as we speak—"

"Tell Madame Geri to send my regards to the spirit world," I said on my way out, not wanting to spoil my writer's high with New Age mumbo jumbo.

I jumped into my truck, eyeing myself in the side mirror for a few brief moments, just to make sure my red curls still looked bouncy and my light makeup still appeared intact before I saw Nick Billie. Of course, nothing completely covered my freckles, but I'd learned to live with them. Sort of. I gave my mouth a quick swipe of pink lip gloss for some added glamour. Kind of.

My hands shook with a nervous tremor as I started up Rusty's engine and cranked on the heater. I was supposed to be asking Nick about Marco's cause of death, but I really wanted to know if he was still speaking to me after the little fiasco last night.

What had gotten into me? Why couldn't I just decide to take up with Cole again or move on to Nick?

Because making a decision has always been my weak spot, a little voice echoed softly inside me. And I didn't really trust that either man was right for me; both of them had commitment problems. *Okay, I'd said it, at least to myself.*

Maybe I'd be better off dating Pop Pop after all. At least I could trust that he'd always be there for me—as long as he was still partially mobile.

Taking in a deep breath, I resolved that this time I would be different. I would take control of the situation and confront Nick about his feelings for me, ask that he forgive me—and demand to know what (or who) killed Marco Santini.

I shoved my truck into gear, and the engine promptly cut off. After pumping the pedal lightly, I tried to start it again—nothing. Just an odd clicking noise.

My take-charge, no-hostages-allowed approach to the men in my life would have to wait. I had to jump-start my battery first.

Typical.

Chapter Five

I called the Island Garage on my cell phone, and without asking, the head mechanic, Stan, arrived twenty minutes later with jumper cables. After the engine had begun to hum, he warned me that if I turned it off again, the battery might not start.

"Bring the truck by my garage today, and I'll put in a new battery for you—at a discount. But it's only a matter of time before this old heap of a truck gives out. If you want to keep it running, you ought to get yourself a man who knows his way around a car engine," Stan advised as he hitched up his pants around his middle-age paunch. The pants promptly settled back under his belt and stayed there, despite a couple more hitching attempts. Muttering an expletive, he threw the cables into the backseat of his aging Buick—the kind with wide seats and a finlike design in the back. *Nice match.*

Still, he had a point about my getting a regular guy in my life who could keep Rusty in working order. I gave

Stan all the money I had with me, five dollars, and drove off with renewed vigor. Using my car psychology, I reasoned that I should try and patch things up with Nick—his Ford F-150 always seemed to be in smooth working order, so that alone made him good boyfriend material. His hard-planed, darkly handsome face didn't hurt either.

Okay, I'd stop at the Coral Island Police Station first, and I prayed to the god of used cars, St. Otto-Mobiles, that Rusty would start up again.

Minutes later, I breezed into the station—a one-story wooden structure on pilings, freshly painted in a pale shade of green, and meticulously landscaped with native plants. A lovely blast of heat greeted me.

Cindy Hinson, Nick Billie's new receptionist (the previous one had moved to Tampa to marry a Greek sponge diver), sat there typing away on her computer. Efficient, with short, spiky hair and a pleasant smile, she nodded in my direction. "How you doing, Mallie?"

"Pretty good." I smiled back and cleared my throat. "Is Detective Billie in?"

"He's on the phone with the medical examiner." She clicked a button, and the printer started up. "Help yourself to some coffee. I just made a fresh pot."

My heart leaped in excitement—both because of the rich coffee aroma that penetrated my thawing nasal cavities and the news that Nick might be getting the lowdown on Marco's cause of death. *Fabu.*

I poured myself a large cup of the dark liquid and inhaled. It had a vague autumn smell, unlike the cheap industrial stuff we brewed in the *Observer* office.

"Pumpkin Spice." Cindy held up her own cup almost like a trophy. "I finally convinced Nick that flavored coffees would make the office seem more appealing."

"I could use a cup back here." A voice trailed out of the back area where the two jail cells were located.

"Tattooed Al?"

She nodded as she moved over to the coffeepot and filled a foam cup. "They caught him biking near the Island Hardware store. I guess his poncho had blown off in the wind, so he was trekking down the main road in nothing but his birthday suit."

"Yikes—in this cold?"

"Yep." She moved toward the cells, shaking her head.

"You've got to be one sick puppy to brave this cold on a bicycle, much less without a stitch of clothing," I replied, curling my hands around the mug to warm them up.

"You can say that again," a deep voice boomed from behind me.

Nick.

Slowly, I turned around, almost afraid to see the contemptuous expression that I had earned with my shoddy behavior last night.

But as my gaze moved toward his face, I felt a jolt of surprise. He simply looked disappointed—and disinterested. *Ouch.*

"I . . . uh . . . wanted to talk with you about an incident yesterday. You know I was having lunch at Little Tuscany when Marco Santini died. Actually, I was sharing a meal with Madame Geri and checking on her son, Jimmy, who, as you know, works as a waiter there. I had the spaghetti, and Madame Geri had pasta. . . ." I took in a deep breath, knowing I was in complete motor-mouth overdrive, but I couldn't stop myself. *Nervous* didn't even begin to describe how I felt at this moment. More like complete, stroke-out anxiety. "Anyway, I saw Marco die, and . . . I was curious to know if you'd heard anything about the cause of death, because it sure looked like he'd had some kind of allergic reaction—"

"Okay, much as I'd like to see you talk yourself into some kind of frenzy," he cut in, rubbing his forehead, "I don't think I can take it right now after the morning I had arresting Al. It took me half an hour to find his poncho before I could even think about allowing him to sit in my truck. Too weird. That would've silenced even your nonstop chattering."

I offered a sheepish smile. "I guess you know me pretty well."

"Not as well as I thought." His eyes darkened.

"Nick, all I can say is I'm sorry—"

"For two-timing me on our date night?"

"That's not exactly true," I protested, standing as tall as I could in my running shoes, so he didn't loom over me. "We aren't exactly dating, and Cole is . . . well, an old friend."

"Really?" Nick watched my face, as if it were some kind of puzzle he couldn't quite figure out.

"Really." I guess I couldn't blame him for being confused. I didn't know how all the pieces fit together either. "Sure, Cole and I were a couple a few years ago, but he left to find himself. Then he reappeared, and now . . . we're just good companions." I forcibly clamped my mouth shut, so I wouldn't say any more. "But we've had a history, and he's fun, and . . ."

He paused, waiting for me to finish, but I didn't know how to complete the thought.

"I get it: you're friends with benefits." He stressed the last word with an ironic tone.

"No way."

Right at that moment, Cindy reappeared. She halted, obviously having heard Nick's comment. She wavered for a few moments. "I'll check back with Al. He might want another cup of coffee—"

"It's okay," Nick said. "We were just about to go into my office, so I could give Mallie a statement for her story." He took my elbow and steered me into the next room, closing the door behind us.

Taking a seat, I sipped my coffee while Nick moved around his desk and flipped through some files. The silence stretched between us like a rubber band, tight and strained.

"Are you actually going to give me a statement about Marco's cause of death?" I finally asked.

"No."

I drained my cup and set it on his desk with a loud thud. "So what was the point in bringing me in here?"

He looked up and caught my gaze. "To make you squirm."

"Okay, I deserved that, but can we at least get back on a more professional footing for now?" I continued, not sure I could take all of this emotional intensity.

"Fine with me." He slapped the files into a neat stack.

He's still bummed out and angry.

Despite the awkwardness, a tiny whisper of delight fluttered inside my heart.

He cares.

Trying to hide my response, I leaned down and retrieved my Official Reporter's Notebook, along with a pen. "Did you get anything from the medical examiner about Marco's death?" I straightened and held the pen poised above my notebook, trying to appear official and ready for business.

He folded his hands on top of the files and said nothing.

"Could you be more specific?" I kidded. "The paramedic told me he likely had anaphylaxis—probably because of some kind of allergic reaction." I tightened my grip on the pen.

Tapping his thumbs together, he still said nothing.

"Can I take that as a 'No comment'?"

"Yes."

Okay, now he's just being stubborn. I chewed on the pen, trying to come up with a tactic that would get Nick to be more forthcoming. I set the ballpoint on his desk. "You know, when I saw Marco stumble out of the kitchen yesterday, he was clawing at his throat and coughing like he was choking. Wouldn't he have known what was happening if he had this kind of extreme allergy?" I grasped my neck with both hands and imitated the gagging reflex that Marco had exhibited, tongue out and coughing. "It kind of looked like that." I repeated the motion.

"Stop. I can't stand to see the replay." He held up a hand. "Look, Mallie, I don't have anything definitive from the medical examiner, except that what the paramedics told you at Little Tuscany was probably Marco's cause of death. The ME said he had hives and a swollen throat, both common for someone with an extreme reaction to shellfish."

"Like shrimp or lobster?" I retrieved my pen again.

He tipped his head in agreement.

"But wouldn't Marco have known that he was allergic to shellfish? Especially because he worked with food for a living."

"I would think so."

"So that means someone might've secretly put shellfish in his food to *cause* the allergic reaction that killed him," I proposed, trying to construct a logical reason for Marco to have eaten shellfish, my thoughts racing a mile a minute.

"That's always a possibility," Nick responded enigmatically.

"It also fits with the incident that occurred at Le Sink last night," I added, half to myself.

His glance sharpened. "What do you mean 'incident'?"

I hesitated. "I was at Le Sink after you and Cole left—"

"Oh, yeah, I heard you took up with Pop Pop as your main squeeze." He gave a snort of laughter.

"How many times do I have to say that I'm *not* dating Pop Pop?" I slapped my thigh for emphasis as the heat of irritation rose to my face. "This damn island grapevine is a creeping weed of misinformation. To think I would date a guy old enough to be my grandfather. Jeez."

"Stranger things have happened." He still sported the vague remnants of a wry smile. "But back to the 'incident.' And please keep it under a thousand words, if possible."

"I'll try." Sarcasm thickened my voice. After gathering my thoughts, I related the particulars of the fight between Guido and Kyle—and my own heroic role in wielding the broom.

Nick scribbled a few notes as I talked.

When I was finished, I peered across his desk and tried to read what he'd jotted down. "Is Guido in trouble?"

"He started a public fight."

"But he didn't really hurt Kyle—"

"I'll talk to both of them." His tone was clipped and final. "Just let me do my job."

"Okay." I pursed my mouth. "But what if Guido was right? Maybe Kyle put the shellfish in Marco's food to poison him. I heard there was some kind of trouble between Kyle's mother and Marco—"

"Mallie"—Nick leaned forward—"I want you to stick to the facts in your story. Francesca Bernini hasn't done anything to warrant her being considered as a suspect."

"So you are initiating an investigation?" I prompted.

"Maybe."

Damn. Back to the one-word answers.

"You've had my statement for the *Observer*," he added.

At least that was a full sentence. "By the way, I'm not exactly writing a news story on Marco's death at Little Tuscany."

"Then what is this interview all about?"

"I'm doing a restaurant review series leading up to 'Taste of the Island,' and the first reviews are covering Le Sink and Little Tuscany—"

"You're now a food critic?" His brow rose in disbelief. "I've never seen you eat anything but fast food and microwave dinners."

"True, but I can tell the difference between fresh grouper and frozen fish sticks," I hastened to add. So what if my palate wasn't gourmet? At least I'd read a copy of the magazine once.

"On a good day," Nick quipped as he leaned back in

his chair, hands behind his head. "What was Anita thinking?"

I rose to my feet with some indignation. "She believes in me—something that would be kind of refreshing from you."

"I guess I'd have to trust you first."

"Trust comes from commitment."

We just stared at each other for a long moment, both knowing we weren't talking about the restaurant reviews any longer. It seemed like we were back at square one, with Nick being cagey and me being disappointed.

Sigh.

I tossed my notebook and pen into my bag. "One last thing: do you think it's strange that Marco died the day after his brother, Carlos, passed away?"

"Conspiracy theory?"

"Nope. Madame Geri prophecy."

"That explains it." He picked up a file. "I have one of these on both brothers, and while they didn't like each other, I don't see anything out of the ordinary about either death." He tossed the file back onto his desk. "Marco's possible allergies aside, Carlos weighed in at the size of a Mack truck and had congestive heart failure. He could barely stand in the ice cream store for more than ten minutes. The poundage and high-fat food aren't exactly a healthy combination—even if he did seem happy all the time."

"True." I remembered his jovial face as he scooped my favorite maple walnut flavor into a sugar cone. He certainly didn't seem like he was stressed, but all of that girth might have been enough to do him in.

Still, Madame Geri's words flitted through my mind. Much as I hated to admit it, she had a sixth sense about untimely deaths—and the kind of secrets that people would do anything to hide.

I heaved my hobo bag strap over my shoulder. "I might talk to Beatrice, just to check on facts for my review, of course."

"Just make sure you keep the conversation about food." He eyed me with a suspicious glint. "And remember, she just lost her father and uncle in the same week."

"I'm not totally insensitive," I said in a defensive tone.

"You could've fooled me."

I pivoted on my heel and left. While Nick's anger might mean he cared about me, it would be a long while before he forgot about being two-timed, as he called it. I had blown it.

Feeling somewhat deflated, I braved the chilly wind and climbed back into my truck. Maybe it was best not to focus so much on my pathetic love life and, instead, figure out what had happened to Carlos and Marco. I might have a better chance of success, that's for sure.

Sending a silent appeal to St. Otto again, I tentatively turned the ignition key. Rusty's engine roared into action. *Yippee.* I guess my saint ally had given me my answer: I had to find the connection between the two brothers' deaths.

Far be it from me to argue with the universe. I'd head

to the Island Garage to get a new battery, and then I'd question Beatrice.

Time to get to work.

Luckily, Stan had a battery to fit the make and model of my ancient rust bucket, so my stop at the garage didn't take too long. While waiting, I texted Sandy to get Beatrice's phone number, then called her to see if I could stop by and chat. When Beatrice hesitated, I told her I worked at the *Observer* and hinted that Guido might need me to be on his side as a witness to the fight at Le Sink.

She immediately acquiesced and gave me the address of her family's house.

It took only a few minutes to get to Beatrice's neighborhood. Located in an older section of the island called Palmetto Place, I quickly pinpointed the midsized stuccoed dwelling that looked like it might have been transplanted from Tuscany. The house was the only one on the street painted the same pink color as the restaurant, with Mediterranean arches across the front facade. The mailbox also had the name SANTINI printed in large letters.

I wasn't an investigative reporter for nothing.

After parking Rusty, I made for the front door. But I didn't even have a chance to knock before Beatrice appeared and let me in. As I entered, I noted that the large living room had a very similar décor to the restaurant: murals with Italian scenes, dark leather furniture, and several wine racks. The same aroma of bread and olive oil even wafted in from the kitchen off to the left.

My mouth watered. It was *way* past lunchtime.

Beatrice quietly shut the door behind me and offered to take my coat. As I gave it to her, I noted her face appeared blotchy from crying.

"How are you doing?" I asked, instantly feeling guilty that food was uppermost on my mind from the moment I stepped inside the house.

"I'm okay, I guess." Her eyes welled up, and she brushed away the tears with the back of her hand. "My older brother is driving down from Jacksonville, so he's going to help with the funeral arrangements. I still can't believe what happened at the restaurant yesterday. Dad was standing there cooking one moment and then choking to death the next—" She broke off, a fresh wave of tears gushing down her cheeks. "It's just a nightmare, especially after losing Uncle C-Carlos two days ago."

"I'm so sorry." I gave her a brief hug. Her thin shoulders felt so delicate, as if they could snap under the weight of her grief.

"The paramedics did everything they could, didn't they?"

"Yes, they did," I assured her.

"It . . . must've been fate." She glanced at a gilt-framed religious picture on the wall and crossed herself, murmuring something under her breath. "Uncle Carlos always said, *'Que sera, sera'*—What will be, will be. And

I guess he was right." She sniffed and shoved her hair back with a resolute hand.

"Guess so."

"Would you like a cup of coffee?" At my eager nod, she motioned me to follow her into the kitchen, which turned out to be a chef's delight: granite countertops, stainless steel double ovens, and a massive glass-fronted refrigerator.

"Amazing." A far cry from my Airstream's minuscule cooking area. "This is an incredible space."

"Dad designed it. He wanted the kitchen to look like the one in the house where he grew up in Tuscany." Her voice sounded wistful. "When I was a little girl, I would stand on a chair while I learned to make homemade pasta with Mom, Dad, and Uncle Carlos. They were all good friends then."

"What happened?"

She paused, coffee scoop in hand. "I don't know. When I was about ten, I came home early from school one day and heard Dad yelling in Italian to Uncle Carlos. I couldn't understand what he was saying. But after that, my uncle didn't hang out with us anymore. My mother never told me what they'd argued about, but I sensed that she knew."

"Your mother was Delores Santini?"

"Uh-huh." Beatrice clicked on the BREW button and then faced me, her delicate features shadowed by even more sadness. "She kept her married name, even though she and my dad divorced years ago."

"And she moved to town after the divorce?" Her eyes widened in surprise. "Where did you hear that?"

"My landlady at the Twin Palms is Wanda Sue."

"'Nuff said." A ghost of a smile raised the corners of Beatrice's mouth. "She was BFFs with my mother; they'd meet at Uncle Carlos' ice cream store for a banana split every Sunday—even after Mom moved to town."

"Interesting." Odd that Wanda Sue had omitted that part when she told me about Delores.

"So your dad didn't get along with your Uncle Carlos for a long time?"

"At least ten years." She pulled two blue-and-white ceramic mugs out of a cabinet. "To tell you the truth, my dad always had an . . . Italian temper. You heard it that day in the restaurant." Her tears seemed to dry up. "I guess everybody just gave in to him, so he wouldn't make a fuss. That's probably what finally drove both Uncle Carlos and my mother to break away from him, even though my uncle stayed on the island."

"So did your uncle ever say what they had argued about?" I restrained myself from grabbing my notebook. It didn't seem respectful.

"No. And I saw him every day before I went into work." Her face softened again. "He was such a cool uncle—caring and patient. He even paid for me to go to culinary school, so I could eventually run the restaurant myself."

"I used to see him at the ice cream store," I replied. "He was always in a good mood, and he gave me extra candy sprinkles on my cone when I'd had a bad day, which occurred almost every twenty-four hours when I first started working at the *Observer*. My editor, Anita, didn't like anything I wrote, and then I had to work for her evil twin sister, Bernice, for a while. She drove me even crazier—" I caught myself, reining in the motor-mouth. Again, it wasn't the time or place.

"Uncle Carlos had a big heart—and maybe that's why his own was giving out: he cared so much about every-one. I . . . I knew he didn't have long to live, 'cause he told me that his heart was failing, and he wouldn't get treat-ment." Her eyes welled up once more. "I loved him to pieces; he was like a second father to me, and he was so good to Guido."

"So your uncle knew he was dying?"

She gave a little nod.

"And he approved of your relationship with Guido, but your father didn't?" I took in a deep whiff of the brewing coffee. *Heavenly.*

"Y-yes," she stammered, all of a sudden more ner-vous than upset. Her hand began to twirl a strand of curly hair, and she inched back from me.

Was Beatrice's display of grief genuine? Certainly, she had loved her uncle, but what about her father? Was she secretly glad he was gone, so he couldn't come be-tween her and Guido? Or maybe she'd had a hand in getting her father out of the picture permanently, since she knew her uncle wouldn't be around long to protect her.

"Um . . . did your father have any food allergies?"

"Y-yes, to shellfish." Beatrice started as if stung by a wasp, but she recovered quickly. "He couldn't even work with shrimp at the restaurant; it would cause a rash to break out on his hands." She poured the coffee, shielding her face with the long fall of her hair. "Why do you ask? Do you think it had anything to do with his death?"

"I don't know for sure, but if your father died of an allergic reaction to something he ate, it's likely that it would be to some kind of shellfish." I took the coffee mug from her. "You know, the fight last night at Le Sink occurred because Guido accused Kyle of harming your father. Do you think he could have managed to put shellfish in something your father ate yesterday?"

"Maybe." She exhaled in a long, drawn-out sigh, as if she'd been holding her breath. "Kyle was at Little Tuscany yesterday morning with his mother. They wanted to go over their menus for 'Taste of the Island.'"

"And?"

Beatrice filled her own cup to the brim and offered me some biscotti. "They never got the chance. As soon as Francesca and Kyle came into the kitchen, my dad started yelling at them about stealing his prized secret sauce recipe. He said he was going to expose Francesca as a food thief."

I raised my hands, palms up. "So?"

She drew back, as though stung for a second time. "She won fifty thousand dollars for that recipe in a national recipe contest; it was enough for her and her son to start up their own Italian restaurant on the island: Taste of Venice. They took a lot of our regular clients."

My mouth dropped open at the amount of money. Maybe I could start whipping up some recipes of my own: Hamburger Helper with mango sauce? Leftover pizza à la mode? They'd be worth about two dollars.

"Anyway, Francesca started yelling back at my dad that his slander was ruining her business and that she would 'take care' of him." Beatrice paused. "Do you think they could've . . . done something to my dad?"

"Were they ever in the kitchen alone?" I took a deep swig of the coffee. *Delish.* My knees grew weak at the scrumptious flavor. "This is really . . . like, incredible coffee, and I drink enough of it to know."

"I ground the beans this morning."

I gulped down the entire cup and then helped myself to a refill. "Okay, back to Francesca and Kyle—so maybe Guido was right about them. They could be suspects."

"But Guido isn't going to get into trouble for saying it, is he?" Her voice turned anxious, and a little frown line appeared between her dark eyebrows.

"Not for the accusation, but maybe the fight. He shouldn't have attacked Kyle, and there were witnesses, including me. To be honest, I had to relate the event to Nick Billie a little while ago." I dipped my own biscotti in the coffee and then took a taste. My knees grew even weaker, causing me to drop into a chair while I gobbled down two more biscotti.

"Detective Billie knows?"

"Yeah . . . sorry."

She slid into a chair across from me. "I don't think Guido even knew what he was doing. We were at the hospital for hours. Then we came back to the island, and Guido took off, saying something in Italian about Kyle. I should have stopped him. Now he's made things worse for himself."

"You mean with his visa?"

She bowed her head and sighed. "He came here as an exchange student but applied for one of those green card lotteries right before he graduated—and won. But until he becomes a full citizen, he has to keep his job and stay out of trouble."

"I think Nick understands that yesterday took its toll on everyone, so I wouldn't worry about Guido, unless there's something else you're not telling me." I ended on a questioning note.

Beatrice's head jerked upward. "No—there's nothing," she said quickly. A shade too quickly.

We sat there for a few moments in silence, and I took a few furtive glances at Beatrice, but she kept her cameo-like features shuttered and closed. Still, a faint pink flush stained her cheeks—a sign that she was hiding something about Guido?

"When is your brother going to come in?" I finally asked.

She checked her filigreed-silver watch. "In about an hour."

"I can stay until then." My cell phone rang, and I checked the caller ID: Sandy. "I need to get this."

As soon as I flipped the cell open, Sandy's voice came through, shrill and anxious, "Mallie, you've got to come back to the office right away. I think they're going to arrest Jimmy!"

Uh-oh.

Chapter Six

W hat?" I clutched my cell phone tighter and rammed it against my ear, trying to make out what Sandy was saying. Her words all jumbled together in a panicked tone, but I thought I made out "locker" and "shellfish" and "Jimmy."

"Sandy, calm down. I can't understand you. Sandy!" The signal cut out. *Damn.* I snapped the cell phone shut. "I'm sorry, Beatrice, but something has come up. I've got to get back to the newspaper office immediately."

"Sure."

I gave her one of my cards. "Call me if you remember anything else about yesterday's . . . uh, events."

She nodded mutely, tears in her eyes again.

I left the house (after grabbing another biscotti) and headed to the *Observer* as fast as Rusty's aging engine would take me. Barely five minutes later, I rushed in the front door of the office and found Sandy standing near Anita's office door, her head on Jimmy's shoulder while he patted her on the back.

110

Jimmy's brow was knit with worry, Sandy's eyes were red-rimmed from crying, and Anita's mouth was drawn tight into a single line of boredom.

"What happened? Did someone else die?" I queried anxiously.

"We couldn't get that lucky," Anita quipped as she leaned against the door frame of her office.

"It's Jimmy," Sandy moaned, raising her head. "He might be arrested because of the shellfish articles found in his locker."

"Whoa." I held up one hand. "Back up and start over—slowly, please." I gestured a "roll 'em" motion with the other hand.

"Let me tell it, sweetheart," Jimmy said, as he dropped a gentle kiss on her head. "One of Nick Billie's deputies came by Little Tuscany today while I was cleaning up the kitchen from yesterday's lunch. After getting my statement, he poked around the whole place, including our staff lockers. Well, inside of mine, he found a couple of online articles about shellfish."

My eyes widened.

"The whole thing was surreal," Jimmy continued. "The deputy took the articles and told me to drop by the police station tomorrow morning to talk with Detective Billie. I don't understand why."

"I already called Madame Geri," Sandy cut in, clinging to Jimmy's arms.

"It doesn't take a psychic to figure that one out," I commented with some asperity. "Nick told me that

Marco Santini died from an allergic reaction—probably to shellfish."

Sandy whimpered and dropped her head back down onto Jimmy's shoulder.

"So, the police think *I* might have put shellfish into food that Marco ate?" Jimmy's words came out slowly as the meaning dawned on him. "But I didn't even know he was allergic to shellfish. And why would I want to kill Mr. Santini?"

"Aside from his being a mean, insensitive, bad-tempered boss?" I queried, as I flashed a significant glance at Anita. She completely missed it because she had begun to slather more bee cream onto her already red, scaly face.

"True, but I've had other bosses just like him," Jimmy admitted, his boy-next-door face baffled.

"Was there any other reason you might be implicated in Marco's death?" I continued.

Sandy raised her head. "What about that money you borrowed from him for our wedding?"

Jimmy paused for a few moments and then jerked his head to one side in disbelief. "But I was paying him back from my wages with thirty-percent interest."

"What?!" I gasped. "That's obscene."

"He told me it was fair, since he paid me a dollar more than minimum wage," Jimmy offered with an open smile. I vowed to have a talk with Madame Geri. Her son was really too trusting. "But I almost had the debt paid off."

"Do you have proof?" I probed.

He grimaced. "No."

"You're even dumber than you look," Anita commented.

"Oh, yeah?" Sandy rushed to the rescue, her face as fierce as that of a mama bear protecting her cubs. "What could be more dumb than slapping some type of bee junk on your face that's making it look like a broiled lobster?"

"Not nearly as dumb as letting some half-baked New Age loon like Madame Geri plan your wedding date—"

"Did somebody mention my name?" The island's freelance psychic stood there in all of her *Happy-Days*-meets-reggae glory: blond dreadlocks, fifties-style outfit—complete with poodle skirt and finely knit sweater—and turquoise parrot, Marley, perched on her shoulder. I had to admire her fashion courage, not to mention the proximity of the bird's sharp beak to her face.

"Yeah, I did." Anita's words sounded defiant, but even she kept a wary eye on Marley.

"The New Age label fits, but I object to being called a 'loon.'" She stared hard at Anita, who stared back, but when Marley began flapping his wings, my boss averted her glance and retreated a few steps. "By the way, Anita, if you keep up with that bee cream, your face is going to puff up like a balloon."

Her hand flew to her face. "It's just filling out the wrinkles."

"I told you, the bees on this island don't produce the right type of honey for human skin." Madame Geri stroked Marley to calm him down. "Your face is rejecting the cream; that's why it's red and swelling."

"Bees are bees, and cream is cream," Anita spat out, but she placed the lid on the jar and screwed it shut. "My skin has never looked better."

Relatively speaking, I added to myself—if you had to choose between a puffy catcher's-mitt face or a sagging saddlebag.

Madame Geri shrugged and turned to her son and Sandy. "Tell me the whole story."

As Sandy repeated what Jimmy had told me, Madame Geri listened intently, occasionally posing a question. Anita took the opportunity to disappear into her office, but I spied her putting another layer of bee cream on her face. *Catcher's mitt, all right.*

"What does it mean, Madame Geri?" Sandy asked. "Is our wedding off because Jimmy is going to j-jail?"

Madame Geri closed her eyes briefly. "I can't tell for sure. We need to find Marco's killer to make certain Jimmy isn't blamed."

"Who said anything about a killer?" I interjected, still eyeing Marley. The bird scared me; in fact, all birds made me slightly uneasy from the time I'd been attacked by a group of maverick ducks near Lake Buena Vista at Disney World. "Maybe Marco could have been cooking up a dish for a customer, and he accidentally swallowed some shellfish."

All three of them turned and looked at me without saying a word.

"Okay, it's a long shot, but it's possible."

"Don't be stupid, kiddo!" Anita shouted from her office.

"Oh, go back to your bee cream!" I yelled back.

Marley flapped his wings again, and I retreated even farther.

"He thought you said 'beak him.'" Madame Geri stroked the bird as she murmured some reassuring words.

"Make sure you translate verbatim for Marley. I don't want my eyes pecked out if he thinks I'm asking him to 'beak' anybody, including me." I kept my tone light but maintained my distance from both of them.

"He understands almost everything." Madame Geri gave the bird one last pat and then returned her attention to Sandy and her son. "Let's say, as I've just heard the spirit world tell me, that Marco was murdered. Who else might be a suspect?" She raised her eyebrows in my direction, waiting for a response.

"All right, here's my two cents' worth: I think Francesca and Kyle might be possibilities. They dropped by Little Tuscany yesterday morning and apparently had a raging argument with Marco. Two hours later, he was dead." I tried to reconstruct the events in my mind, wondering how mother and son could have managed to slip shellfish into food that Marco was cooking. "Who else was in the kitchen during the morning, Jimmy?"

"Let me think." Jimmy tapped his chin. "Uh, aside from Francesca and Kyle, and Beatrice and Guido—just me." He swallowed audibly. "That doesn't sound so good, does it?"

I tried to offer an encouraging smile, but I had to agree with him. Potential Marco killers weren't exactly coming out of the woodwork. "Why did you have the shellfish articles in your locker?"

"I was working on some new recipes for Mr. Santini that included shrimp and lobster," Jimmy explained. "So I was reading up on the difference between freshwater and saltwater shrimp, and Maine lobster and Florida lobster— that kind of thing. Honest. I just wanted to be a better cook for Mr. Santini, not kill him with shellfish."

"I believe you, Jimmy," I said.

"Sounds lame to me!" Anita shouted out again. Sandy went over and closed the door to her office.

"What do we do now?" Jimmy circled his arm around Sandy again when she came back to stand by him. "I want to make sure that the wedding takes place, and that won't happen if I'm arrested."

"You're not going to be arrested, son," Madame Geri pronounced in a firm tone. "We just need to come up with a plan to smoke out the murderer." They all looked at me again.

"Oh, *please*. The last time I got involved with a mysterious death, the killer drenched me in mango pulp right before she tried to silence me forever."

Never again.

The little group kept up the stare-fest, including Marley, who drilled me with his beady little eyes. I don't know if it was fear or foolishness, but I found myself agreeing to help with the "plan."

"Jimmy and I can go to Le Sink and try to get info out of Kyle," Sandy offered, sending a beaming smile up at Jimmy. "We'll be like that private-detective couple in the old black-and-white movies—"

"Nick and Nora Charles," I finished for her, not wanting to point out that Sandy and Jimmy's wholesome, middle-American appearance didn't exactly jibe with the hard-drinking, sophisticated 1920s style of Dashiell Hammett's duo.

Still, what they lacked in cosmopolitan canniness, they made up for with eager honesty—not to mention desperation over Jimmy's possible jailbird future.

"Mallie and I will go to Taste of Venice and see what we can glean from Francesca," Madame Geri volunteered. "You can also get a restaurant review out of it."

"That one isn't on my list," I protested, not wanting to be saddled with Madame Geri for another meal.

"Put it on the list, kiddo!" Anita yelled out one more time. *Jeez, does she have superhuman hearing or what?*

"Great," Sandy enthused. "You guys will be like Thelma and Louise."

"They weren't detectives—just two women on a crazy joyride," I clarified. "And they wound up dead at the end of the film."

"Oh." Sandy's mouth puckered in concern. "Maybe you could just be yourselves, then."

I glanced at Madame Geri with her dreadlocks and

parrot; yeah, being herself was probably best. Then I looked down at my worn jeans and misshapen sweater, realizing I was probably most comfortable being my shabby-chic self too.

"I need to go home and walk Kong before dinner."

"I'll book the reservation and take Marley home." Madame Geri set the parrot on Sandy's desk. After giving him a few pats, she whipped out her cell phone and began clicking on the keys. "Mallie, you'd better dress up. This restaurant isn't another Le Sink."

I felt a touch of excitement flicker inside. "You mean it's a nice place?"

"Four stars, according to some of the spirits who ate there when they were alive."

"Cool," Jimmy said with a smile. "Maybe they can suggest an entrée."

Too freaky. I refused to take food advice from dead people. I had to draw the line somewhere.

By the time I returned to my Airstream at the Twin Palms RV Resort, the temperature had begun to drop again, and the air had taken on a sharp chill. Quickly, I hustled Kong out for a quick walk and took a peep at Cole's van before I retreated inside my silver hutlike home.

It looked empty and dark. And still no sign of Cole.

I sighed.

"It's no more than I deserve, Kong," I commented to my teacup poodle as I hiked up the thermostat. Holding my breath, I waited to see if the heater clicked on.

Nada.

I switched on Pop Pop's space heater, hoping it would keep chugging through the night. I flipped on the television and saw Miss Perky Weathergirl predict that the cold snap would last at least a week. *Not good.* I left another message for Sam, begging him to come over and fix my heater, though I figured he had about fifty similar calls from islanders panicked at the thought of nothing but a twenty-nine-dollar space heater between them and frostbite.

Coral Islanders never prepared for chilly weather and, consequently, feared it almost more than a hurricane.

I freshened up, plumping up my red curls (my best feature), smoothing on a thin layer of makeup over my freckles (my worst feature), and gliding a dab of pink lipstick onto my lips (my okay feature). Then I had a more problematic decision: what to wear to a fancy restaurant.

Aside from my jeans and tops, I possessed only two dresses: a yellow sundress that I'd picked up at Secondhand Rose, the island's consignment shop, and a longsleeved black jersey dress, which my lawyer-sister had given me years ago and I'd never worn. Too preppy for my taste.

I guess the decision wasn't that hard. I could either freeze in a sundress or be comfortable in my sister's conservative castoff. As I slipped on the black dress, I heard a knock at my door.

Cole? Nick?

My heart leaped with joy. Maybe one or both of them had forgiven me.

I finished dressing, slipped into a pair of pumps, also a gift from my sister, and caught sight of myself in the bedroom mirror. *Not bad.* Black made my red curls turn almost copper and my skin look almost creamy.

I swung open the door and beheld Pop Pop.

The joy faded like the last rays of a setting sun.

"Just checking to see if that space heater was still working." He pulled down his knit cap to cover his ears; he looked like a hip-hop mummy.

"It's fine." I tried to hide my disappointment behind a bright smile. "I'm hoping Sam will come over some-time tonight and fix the heater, so I can return your portable one by morning."

"It's yours as long as you need it." He squinted and pulled out a pair of thick, Coke-bottle glasses. "You look mighty nice, Mallie. Are we going out to dinner again? I can be ready in two shakes."

"No need to shake anything." I shook my head. "I have to do a restaurant review with Madame Geri to-night, so it's a . . . uh . . . business dinner."

"Okay." His saggy features drooped in disappoint-ment, which meant his chin hit his skinny chest. "I under-stand, and I don't want you to feel bad about ditching me. I mean, I know I'm not exactly a spring chicken, while you're a cute chick."

Talk about laying a major guilt trip on me—and it

was working. "I guess we could include another person for dinner," I said with slow reluctance.

"Great! I'll be waiting for you to pick me up, tootsie." He grinned, which, unfortunately, caused his dentures to shift out of place. "Oops."

As he snapped the dentures back into place and hobbled off, I closed the door. Kong nuzzled my ankle and gave a supportive yelp, which I swear hit a note that seemed almost human.

Oh, boy. This should make for a fun evening of companionship—the geriatric RV park caretaker and island psychic. Could my heart take it?

I slipped on my old coat, hopped into my truck, and headed for Pop Pop's cottage.

Just call me the dating diva.

Chapter Seven

By the time we arrived at the Taste of Venice restaurant, it was an hour later. I'd had to drive back to the Twin Palms RV park twice—first for Pop Pop's spare oxygen tank and, second, for his blood-pressure medication. Madame Geri was standing out front, pointing at her watch. She'd changed into her evening dress as well: a 1920s-style sequined tunic, leggings, and a cape.

Sassy, if not classy.

The restaurant stretched behind her, a smallish wooden structure with a vine-covered trellis across the front and twinkling lights circling the windows. It had a laid-back, cozy feel, the kind of ambiance that only a really good restaurant could pull off successfully.

"Sorry we're late," I said, "but Pop Pop had a few last-minute items he'd forgotten." I helped him out of my truck, now being an expert at handling him and his oxygen paraphernalia.

As we approached, Madame Geri whispered, "Don't

get too attached; he's got a date with destiny soon—if you get my drift."

I started. "How soon?"

"A few years." She shrugged. "You've got time to be a couple, but don't expect a long-term relationship."

"We're not dating," I hissed back as we entered Taste of Venice. The subdued lighting and fine linens bore out the quiet elegance of the exterior. "It's just that he gave me a space heater, and I felt sorry for him, because he's all alone every night. I know how it feels, now that both of my potential boyfriends have disappeared—" I broke off, realizing how lame I sounded. "All right, fine, we're dating! I'm dating a man in his eighties!"

Everyone in the restaurant fell into silence right at the moment I spewed forth with my loud declaration. I raised my chin, refusing to be embarrassed, until I spied Cole and Nick in the group of diners at a table together.

Huh?

I heard a few snickers, which I tried to ignore, and eventually people resumed their conversations.

My two MIA boyfriends had just heard me say that I was now dating a man old enough to have known President Roosevelt personally.

Still cringing, I realized the bigger question was, what were they doing at the same table? Were they double-dating already, and the women had excused themselves for a few moments? Had they each found someone to replace me within twenty-four hours?

Then again, I was with Pop Pop.

Wishing the floor would swallow me up, I tried to keep up a good front and a firm hold on Pop Pop's oxygen tank.

A middle-aged woman with a fall of thick, chestnut hair, chic glasses, and a stunning black suit came up, carrying a stack of menus. "I'm Francesca, the owner, and it's a pleasure to finally meet you, Madame Geri."

My companion gave a regal nod of her dreadlocks. She'd pinned them up for the evening and had placed a jeweled comb in the back, keeping with her 1920s theme.

Francesca turned to me. "And I understand you are the food critic from the *Observer*. It's a pleasure to meet you and . . . uh . . . your date."

"I'm Pop Pop Welch," he chimed in. "Mallie and I are really just friends, but I'm hoping for something more permanent, if you get my drift."

"Of course," Francesca answered, without altering her smoothly professional manner. "May I seat you at one of our best tables?"

"As long as it's not a booth." Pop Pop tapped his oxygen. "I can't replace the tank fast enough if I'm not in a chair."

"Certainly, sir." Again, she didn't miss a beat.

Boy, she had that class-act down—no doubt born of long practice—which was probably the best description of her job.

As she led us through the dining room, I shot a furtive glance in Cole and Nick's direction. They appeared to be deep in conversation and didn't even look up as we moved toward our table.

I coughed and cleared my throat loudly as I went by them, hoping to get their attention, but they didn't so much as blink.

What was up?

Stopping to look at them again, I didn't realize Pop Pop had taken a little pause to catch his breath, and I rammed into him, causing him to stumble into a table. A glass of water tipped over and shattered on the tile floor. At that point, Nick and Cole switched their attention to our motley trio making our way across the dining room. Nick started to rise, but Francesca held up a hand in his direction.

"I'll have it cleaned up—please just continue with your dinner."

Nick sank back down. *Damn.* Now I'd never know what they were talking about.

I steadied Pop Pop by grasping his arm and then steered him along behind Francesca. He moved with the speed of a turtle, but we finally made it to our table without further incident.

After we took our seats, with Pop Pop next to me, Francesca handed us paper-thin menus that apparently contained only five items, none of which had prices.

"How much are the entrées?" I asked, mentally calculating what I'd have to pony up beyond the twenty bucks Anita had promised per meal.

Francesca peered down her patrician nose and mentioned an amount that caused me to catch my breath.

"I'll get the check," Madame Geri offered, much to my relief. I didn't even make a pretense of arguing with her over it, because I knew it wouldn't be yours truly. I didn't carry that much cash, nor did I have that much money available on my debit card.

"Thanks," I said, after Francesca moved away to clean up Pop Pop's accident. "So, what do you think, Madame Geri?"

"I'll have the lobster ravioli with the secret sauce," she pronounced after scanning the menu.

"No, I mean, do you think Francesca is the type of person who could've murdered Marco?" I watched the imperious way Francesca flicked her hand to motion over a waiter to sweep up the broken glass. "She certainly seems to rule this place like Lucrezia Borgia—which sort of fits, even though the shellfish wasn't exactly a poison."

"I don't know yet, but I'm getting a powerful vibe that tells me she's capable of strong emotion—the kind that can drive a person to kill." She tucked a rogue dreadlock behind her ear, her mouth pursed in thoughtful reflection. "But whether she did it or not remains to be seen."

"Did what?" Pop Pop tapped his hearing aid. "My hearing aid must be on the fritz."

"Uh . . . change the menu," I stammered, not liking to lie, even to protect Pop Pop from hearing things that could cause his pacemaker to short circuit.

"I thought I heard the word *murder,*" he continued,

pulling out the left hearing aid and replacing the battery with a backup he kept in his pocket. "Ah, that's better; now I can hear everything."

Madame Geri and I exchanged a warning look and focused on our menus.

"Since I have to review the food, let's all order a different entrée," I suggested.

"Huh? I don't need a tray." Pop Pop tapped the right hearing aid this time. "Dadgum it, now the other one went out, and I have only one replacement battery."

"Entrée!" I repeated, smiling inwardly. *Good.* Now he only could hear every other word. "How about you order the mushroom risotto, Pop Pop, and I'll have the *shrimp* Alfredo?" I stressed the shellfish word with a knowing nod in Madame Geri's direction.

"Good choice." She winked at me.

Our waiter approached in his tuxedo, white cloth over his arm, and took our order with a formal gravity reserved for high tea at the Ritz. After last night's debacle at Le Sink, though, it was kind of refreshing.

Once he left, I leaned forward toward Madame Geri. "Did you see who was sitting together over there? Nick and Cole?"

"Uh-huh." She folded her hands on the table. "Mallie, you tried to date both of them at the same time; they're probably commiserating."

"Hah." I didn't turn around. "They don't look inconsolable to me."

"You don't know that."

"I guess not." I pretended to drop my napkin on the floor and tilted my face in their direction as I retrieved it. *Commiserating, my eye.* They appeared lost in pleasant conversation.

Double hah.

Pop Pop reached for his water and, remembering what had happened at Le Sink with his dentures, I moved the glass out of his reach. "Why don't we have some wine?"

"Sure, toots." He draped a bony arm across the back of my chair. I leaned as far away from him as I could get without moving to the other side of the table.

"Yes, let's order a bottle." Madame Geri gave a little wave in Francesca's direction, who, having finished overseeing the cleanup, instantly returned to our table. This food critic thing wasn't half-bad; I did get incredible service.

"We'd like to order a bottle of pinot noir," Madame Geri said, scanning the wine list for a few moments. "Let's go with the Torrini vineyard. It seems to be one of your better vintages."

Francesca nodded in agreement. "Or you might try the Armanti merlot."

"Wouldn't the pinot noir complement your special sauce better?" Madame Geri asked, folding her hands into a bridge and leaning her chin on top, her eyes on Francesca. "The menu says the sauce has a five-herb blend. . . . What are they?"

"Oregano, basil, Italian parsley, and two other ingredients."

Madame Geri lifted her eyebrows, waiting for our hostess to finish the list.

"I can't tell you what the other ingredients are—it's a house specialty."

Francesca seized the wine list but couldn't budge it from under Madame Geri's elbows. "Could you let me have the wine list? Then I'll get your pinot noir." Geri smiled, elbows firmly planted.

"I bet I know," Pop Pop remarked, a twinkle in his eye. "It's dried cheese out of one of those cans. You know, the stuff you shake on pizza."

Glaring at him, Francesca placed one hand on her hip. "Do you mean parmesan?"

"Yeah, that's it!" Pop Pop threw his hands up in excitement. "Gimme an extra shake on my sauce."

"I don't use canned parmesan cheese, either in my special sauce or other entrées. Everything that we serve is homemade, fresh to order, with *nothing* canned." The glare turned almost murderous.

I drew back into the circle of Pop Pop's cadaver-like arms.

"Now, may I have my wine list?" The irritation in Francesca's voice upped a notch.

"Sure." Madame Geri held it out and sat back. Francesca whipped the wine list away from her and stalked off.

"What was that all about?" I inquired in a hushed tone.

"Just pushing her a bit." Madame Geri opened her retro bag and produced a silver compact. As she powdered her nose, she commented, "By the way, I'm still trying to commune with Anita's ancestors about your raise."

"And?"

"Still nothing. But I haven't given up yet." Madame Geri slipped the compact back into her purse. "I have my ways of finding things out."

I couldn't argue with that one. Right then, a youngish, Latin-looking guy with a guitar started playing classical music on the tiny stage. Diverted, I listened to the dreamy romantic song, wishing that either Cole or Nick sat at my table, rather than the one-thousand-year-old man and the loopy island psychic.

In a short time, our food arrived, and I inhaled the garlic and herb aroma that wafted up from my shrimp Alfredo. My mouth began to water in anticipation of biting into one of those jumbo shrimp.

Maybe this dinner wouldn't be so bad after all.

Pop Pop took his napkin, carefully unfolded it, and tucked it into his shirt collar, bib-style. "I forgot my glasses—blast it!"

Then he grabbed a fork and tried to spear a giant mushroom in the middle of the risotto. He missed, and the mushroom went flying off his plate and smack into Francesca, as she approached with our wine.

She halted, staring down at the large red blob of sauce that stained her white suit. Muttering a loud expletive, she turned to Madame Geri. "You did that on purpose—"

"It was Pop Pop," I cut in. "He's got arthritis in his hands."

"Liar!" she spat out. "This is a designer suit, and I demand that you pay for the cleaning bill."

"Not likely." Madame Geri calmly began to sample her own entrée, ignoring Francesca's hissy fit.

Sensing that things might come to head, I shoveled in as much of my entrée as I could and took a couple of quick bites of Pop Pop's risotto. No matter what, I'd have to write a restaurant review, so I needed to have some idea of the food quality at Taste of Venice.

The risotto melted in my mouth with an explosion of taste so strong, if I'd been standing, my knees would've gone weak at the delicate blend of Italian flavors.

Wow.

In the meantime, Pop Pop kept trying to spear mushrooms, which flew off his plate like Frisbees, hitting Francesca in the chest, whapping a middle-aged guy at the next table, and slamming into his female companion, knocking her silver wig askew.

The woman gasped and tried to straighten her cheap synthetic bouffant, but then it tilted to the other side and looked even worse.

"Stop that, old man!" Francesca shouted, holding her hands up to ward off any more wayward mushrooms.

"Don't call him 'old,'" I said in a huff. I might refer to him as an "aging dotard," but I was his date for the evening.

"This is *my* restaurant, and I can do what I want."

Francesca tried to snatch the fork out of Pop Pop's hand, but he evaded her attempts.

Madame Geri didn't attempt to halt Pop Pop's mad attack on the mushrooms. Instead, she held up a forkful of lobster and commented, "I think I know what's in this secret sauce."

"Shut up." Francesca slammed the wine bottle onto our table and tried to remove Pop Pop's plate, but he edged it away from her. "You know nothing about my fifty-thousand-dollar sauce."

"Did Marco?" Madame Geri countered. "It was *his* recipe, wasn't it?"

Francesca's eyebrows lowered in a thunderous line. "How dare you accuse me of stealing? You're nothing but a phony psychic who hangs out with a girl who works for a two-bit paper and an old fossil who can barely chew his own food."

I stopped midbite. She was really hitting below the belt. "Hey, the *Observer* might not be the *Washington Post,* but a lot of islanders read it, and a bad review would hurt your business." I slammed down my fork. "And Pop Pop *can* chew his food if he's wearing his dentures."

She turned on me. "You can shut the hell up too."

I opened my mouth, starting to phrase a pithy retort, but noticed Nick Billie coming over. I clamped my lips together and remained silent.

"I don't care if you're doing a review of my restaurant. I want you all out of here." Francesca raised her chin and pointed at the front door. "Now!"

"Okay, everyone, just calm down," Nick said as he approached. "No one has to leave."

Goody. I still had two shrimp left and hated to let the food go to waste.

"We were just enjoying a pleasant dinner when Francesca started shouting." Madame Geri dabbed her napkin on Pop'Pop's lips. "I think she's deranged."

Francesca shrieked and attempted to throttle Madame Geri, but Nick seized her arm and pulled her back.

People stopped talking, preferring to enjoy the show at our table, and for a mad moment, I wondered if I could hide under the linen cloth. I couldn't take another restaurant scene, especially with Nick struggling to hold back the owner's fury, which Madame Geri had unleashed.

Just then, Guido rushed into the dining room, fastening a wild gaze in Francesca's direction and hollering, "Murderer! You killed Mr. Santini!"

Oh no. Here we go again.

Chapter Eight

Guido headed, arrow-straight, for Francesca, whose flailing arms flapped against Nick's restraining hold like the wings of a trapped bird.

As Guido grew closer to his target, I stood up, not sure what to do. Checking my companions, I noticed that Madame Geri remained seated, and Pop Pop was still occupied with spearing a mushroom with his fork.

Not much help there.

"Do you need help?" I finally managed to ask Nick, not sure whether to abandon my lone shrimp or kick Francesca in the shin.

"I've got it under control," he responded in a grim tone, somehow managing to clamp down on Francesca's arms.

When Guido reached us, Nick held up a hand. "Stop right there, or I'm arresting all of you."

Guido halted. Francesca froze. No one else in the dining room batted an eye, including me.

"I finally got one!" Pop Pop raised his fork with a small mushroom poised on the prongs.

Yippee.

"I want all of you outside—now," Nick ordered, gesturing at our little group with a circular motion of his hand. Abashed, we all trooped behind him like a line of soldiers following orders.

Before I abandoned my shrimp Alfredo, I grabbed my coat; something told me we might be out there for a good long while. Then I helped Pop Pop to his feet, secured his oxygen tank, and assisted him as he shuffled across the dining room.

We passed Cole, but he didn't look up. *Still mad at me, I guess.*

Once Pop Pop and I made it out the door, I noticed that Francesca had already begun relating to Nick her side of the dispute with Madame Geri, but the island psychic managed to counter every point with the flair of a fighter in combat. Guido stood to one side, arms folded, not speaking.

While the female gladiators continued their verbal jabs, Nick lowered his head and scratched the back of his neck. Eventually, when they showed no sign of abating, he raised his head again. "This isn't getting us anywhere."

"You're telling me," Pop Pop protested, still clutching his fork with the elusive mushroom. "All I wanted was a quiet dinner with my girl." He pointed at me, and I managed a shaky smile in return, not sure what was more embarrassing: my "date's" touching attraction to me or sense of pride over his spearing the mushroom.

"Sorry about that," Nick said. I detected barely restrained humor in his voice, and that caused me to cringe even more.

"I'll get over it." Pop Pop gulped the mushroom and swallowed it whole.

I waited to see if I'd have to give him the Heimlich maneuver, but he seemed okay.

"All right, here's what we're going to do," Nick began, focusing on Beatrice's boyfriend first. "Guido, you go home, and stay there. I don't want any more outbursts from you. Got it?"

The young man nodded, staring down at his shoes. *"Sì."*

"Francesca and Madame Geri, you two need to just cool it. There's no point in arguing about a recipe when Marco isn't around to care."

"He cares, trust me." Madame Geri pronounced. "Just because he's crossed over doesn't mean he's not connected with what's going on."

Francesca drew back and crossed herself as if to ward off some evil.

Did she have something to fear? Maybe—if she killed Marco.

Nick raised an eyebrow. "Okay, let's just say he doesn't care from *this* world."

"Fine." Madame Geri inclined her head. "If you want to limit your *doors of perception.*"

I shivered, partly from the cold, partly from the thought that Marco might be hovering around the Taste of Venice, and partly from the fact that Madame Geri actually could quote from Blake's *The Marriage of Heaven and Hell.*

"So, I want everyone to hit the road and forget about what happened here tonight," Nick said. "Do I make myself clear?"

More nods from the group.

As they made for their cars, I lingered, along with Pop Pop.

"I'm freezing my buns off," Pop Pop announced, his dentures beginning to chatter. Not an appealing sight.

"I'll take you home," Madame Geri said, motioning him over to her vehicle. I could have cried in gratitude, as I helped him wheel his oxygen tank over to my new best friend, Madame Geri. Once he was settled in the passenger seat, I gave her a thumbs-up.

"Pretty good evening, huh?" Madame Geri leaned over and whispered to me. "We now know that Francesca has the temperament to commit murder."

"You mean, you said all that just to get her annoyed?" My mouth dropped open in amazement.

"Oh yeah."

"Hey, ladies, don't fight over me." Pop Pop leaned back in the seat with a smug quirk to his mouth. "I've got my Social Security check coming in the mail tomorrow, and the rest of the week is open to kick up my heels with you."

And break a hip on your way down, I added silently.

"He's all yours." I tapped the top of Madame Geri's car and stepped back.

As she drove off, I sensed Nick was standing behind me. The wind had started to whip up with a biting chill, but I could still catch a whiff of Nick's deep-woodsy after-shave. I shivered again, but this time for a different reason.

"How can you pass up an offer like Pop Pop's?" His voice held a thread of humor again.

Slowly, I turned around, and our eyes met. "It's hard— the oxygen and dentures are a potent combination."

"Why were you and Madame Geri here tonight?"

"Uh . . . for my new gig as the *Observer* food critic. You know what a slave-driver Anita can be about get-ting stories out, and with 'Taste of the Island' coming up this weekend, she wants as many reviews posted to the blog as I can do—lunch and dinner. Can you believe that? I never ate much more than a sub or microwave dinner in my Airstream, but now I . . . I—" I broke off, my teeth beginning to chatter as the cold supercharged my motormouth.

"Let's get out of this wind." He took my arm and drew me back toward the front of the building.

That cut some of the breeze, though I wrapped my arms around myself to contain the maximum amount of warmth. Nick halted next to me, so close I could feel his body heat. *Be still, my heart.*

"So, this was just an innocent dinner with Madame Geri, and you weren't here trying to get some kind of confession out of her that she murdered Marco Santini?"

Damn.

"I'll take your silence as a yes."

"Maybe—okay, it's true. We're all worried at the *Observer* that Jimmy might get jailed because of the shellfish articles found in his locker," I blurted. There was no point in trying to hide anything from Nick; he knew me too well.

"I'm not arresting Jimmy, but he does need to explain those articles."

"He was researching new ways to cook shrimp at the restaurant."

"It sounds plausible, I guess."

"You don't sound convinced."

"Mallie, I have to pursue all leads when it's a case like this one."

My ears perked up, and I gazed at him with pleading eyes. "So it *is* a murder investigation? I need to know—for Jimmy's sake."

He sighed, an echo that floated toward me in the wind. "I can't say for sure. Marco definitely died from a reaction to shellfish, and since he knew about his allergy, it seems unlikely that he would knowingly eat any kind of shellfish."

"So someone put it in his sauce?" *Just as I had thought.*

"Seems so."

"What about Carlos' death? Is there a connection?"

He shook his head. "Carlos Santini died of a heart attack. His cardiologist told me that he had given Carlos only days to live after his last visit. He simply went home, apparently knowing he would die."

"Really? That feels wrong to me, especially because

he loved Beatrice so much." The wind began to howl, almost like a wail for the lost lives of the Santini brothers.

"Something else feels wrong." Nick leaned one arm against the wall and lowered his face to a level inches from my own.

My breath caught in my throat, as my heart began to beat with a nervous staccato. "I . . . I . . . uh . . . don't know what you mean."

"Yes, you do." His dark eyes turned into liquid fire, burning through me. "You can't just dangle Cole and me as if we were toys. You've got to choose."

The staccato turned into a pounding allegro. "I've known Cole for a long time, and I can't just pretend that we weren't a couple."

"He's the past?"

"Sort of." Okay, now I was making a total muddle of this whole conversation, but I couldn't think straight when Nick stood this close to me. "Is that what you were talking to him about?"

"Worried that we might start a fistfight with Pop Pop over you?" One side of his mouth turned up with amusement. "Nothing so dramatic. I just ran into him inside the restaurant when he was taking pictures for Francesca, and I asked if he would do mug shots for me."

"Oh." A tiny tug of disappointment pulled at my heart. Silly, I know.

"But I would fight him for you." Nick voice deepened.

"Pop Pop or Cole?"

"Both." He lowered his mouth and covered mine with a searing kiss that went on and on and on. My arms slipped around his waist, and I leaned into the hard planes of his body. Desire flooded through me, stronger than anything I'd known, pulling me into emotional depths and raw feelings.

Whoa.

I pulled back, gulping the cold air as if I had just run a marathon. "Nick, this is too much. . . . I need some time."

He searched my face, his own breathing ragged. "You can take an hour, a day, or a month, but you can't hide from what's between us. I know, because I've been trying to do that from the moment I set eyes on you. It just grows more consuming."

Go for it, a tiny voice whispered inside me.

Why not?

My hands slipped around his neck, drawing Nick's face down to mine again, right at the moment when I heard the front door of the Taste of Venice open. Some sixth sense caused me to turn away from Nick—and catch sight of Cole.

For once, I was speechless. It felt like a replay of last night when both men had appeared at my Airstream, and I couldn't find the words to express what I was feeling. I just didn't know.

"I didn't mean to interrupt," Cole said in a voice full of hurt.

"You weren't," I hastened to answer. "We were just talking about the upcoming 'Taste of the Island.'" *Lame.*

"Sure." Cole disappeared back into the restaurant, and I flinched at the shadow of distress that had passed across his normally upbeat face.

"Mallie—" Nick began.

"I've got to go. My heater is on the blink, and I need to make sure that Sam fixes it tonight, since there's a hard-freeze warning." Before he could respond, I dashed for my truck, started the engine, and got the heck out of there.

As I drove away, I checked in my rearview mirror; Nick just stood there, watching me drive off. For a few mad moments, I toyed with the idea of jerking the wheel in the opposite direction and taking up where Nick and I had left off.

But I was scared—really scared. And I couldn't just dump Cole. We had a history. And since he'd come to Coral Island, I remembered how much fun we used to have when we were a couple in Orlando, despite my days spent sweeping litter at Epcot.

I headed north on Cypress Drive, trying to push all thoughts of Nick and Cole out of my mind. I couldn't deal with the dueling boyfriends right now; it was too confusing, too painful, too exciting. Especially when I had more important things looming, like finding Marco's killer before Jimmy was jailed.

Focus. My hands tightened on the wheel, and I straightened in my seat and mulled over the paucity of suspects.

Francesca certainly had the temperament of someone who might commit a crime of passion, but maybe she wasn't calculating enough to plan a murder. Her son, Kyle, didn't seem capable of planning his day, much less an elaborate plot to poison someone.

That left Jimmy; I knew he didn't do it. And Guido didn't appear to be much more than a volatile kid besotted with his first love.

No one else had access to the kitchen the day that Marco died—except Beatrice. And I didn't believe that she could harm her own father. He might have been a bit of a tyrant, but she'd loved him; that much was pretty clear.

So that left me with . . . no suspects.

I bit my lip in frustration. I was missing something, but what?

All of a sudden, something hit my windshield, smashing against the glass. My hands flew up to cover my face, causing Rusty to veer into the left lane. I grabbed the wheel and jerked it to the right as I pumped the brakes, but I was going too fast. My truck careened onto the shoulder, moving ever closer to a massive palm tree.

I'm going to die.

No!

Steer into the skid, I suddenly remembered from my high school defensive driving class.

Instantly, I yanked the wheel in the opposite direction, and miraculously, my truck righted itself, and I slowly brought it to a halt on the side of the road.

Hands shaking and heart pounding, I tried to take stock of what had happened. Luckily, the glass hadn't shattered—just cracked, with jagged threads stretching across the entire windshield. Could I have hit an animal and caused it to flip up onto the truck? Or had a bird dive-bombed my truck?

I checked on both sides of my vehicle. Nothing. Then my glance drifted to the side mirror and what might be behind Rusty.

A large coconut lay in the middle of the road.

I gasped. It was certainly big enough to have done that kind of damage to the glass, but how could it have dropped onto my truck when the tree was on the side of the road?

Just then, a car streaked out of the saw palmetto brush with its lights off and raced in the opposite direction. Before I could see the license plate, it was gone.

I jumped out the door, trying at least to catch the make and model in the dark.

Oh, hell, too late!

Kicking the toe of my pumps on the shell road in frustration, I took one last look around and climbed back into my truck. Then, as I fastened my seat belt, I started shaking again as the reality of my near brush with death set in.

Someone had tried to kill me.

After several attempted calls to Sandy, Wanda Sue, and Madame Geri—yes, I was that upset—I finally had enough strength to head back to the Twin Palms RV Resort. I drove slowly, very slowly, almost like one of the aging tourists that I mocked for driving at a snail's pace.

Eventually, I arrived home and parked in front of my Airstream, thankful that I was still alive. Someone had deliberately thrown that coconut at my windshield, hoping that I would be driven off the road and injured, maybe even fatally.

But who?

Marco's killer?

Now my legs began to shake as well.

I tilted my head back and closed my eyes, taking in a few deep, calming breaths. Once I had the trembling under control, I took a cautious peep around my RV site. Cole's van remained—still and dark—on one side, and on the other side, there appeared to be . . . the old Airstream. Dull and dingy, for sure. The shadow trailer echoing the silver, hutlike appearance of my own.

I tried to pinpoint more details about it, until a rap on the window startled me out of my reverie.

I glanced to the left and spied Wanda Sue.

Whew. A friendly face.

I climbed out of the truck and flung my arms around

her in a huge hug of relief. "I'm so glad to see you!" I exclaimed, with a catch in my throat.

"Oh, honey, what's wrong?" Wanda Sue tilted her head and gave me a speculative once-over. And that was no mean task while keeping her giant teased beehive hairdo intact in the strong wind.

"I think someone just tried to kill me." I burst into tears.

"What!?" Her hand flew to her mouth. "Are you sure?"

I pointed at my cracked windshield.

"Lordy." She put an arm around my shoulders. "Let's get you out of this cold."

Wanda Sue at my side, we made for the Airstream door. As I fumbled with my key, I noticed that the twin of my trailer, which I had just seen, was no longer there. I paused, brushing the tears from my cheeks and blinking to clear my vision. *I know it was there.* "W-what happened to the Airstream parked next door? It was back."

"I didn't see anything."

"That old Airstream—it's gone, but I thought I saw it right there again." I pointed at the now-empty site.

Wanda Sue patted me on the arm. "No one checked in—trust me. But someone did drop by earlier." She snatched up the note that had been taped to my door.

I fixed your heater. Namaste, Sam.

"Yahoo! Sam is the best."

"What's that 'name mast' thing?"

"Yoga-speak. It means 'peace.'"

Wanda Sue frowned, then shrugged. "I don't get all of that Bubba stuff."

Did she mean Buddha*?* As I opened the door, Kong flung himself at me, barking and licking my face with an enthusiasm unparalleled by anyone else in my life. I pressed him to me and sighed happily. My pooch's adoration remained the one sane and stable thing in my life.

"Let me walk him. You get changed and relax." Wanda Sue took Kong's leash and said, "Hey, little guy." She leveled a stern glance at him; he promptly began to gnaw on her sequined shoes.

"He doesn't like being called the *L* word," I said.

"Pffffft. If the shoe fits, honey, you have to wear it with pride." She exited the Airstream, tugging on Kong's leash while he nipped at her legs, ankles, and feet.

That Wanda Sue is a real friend.

I dragged myself to the back of my Airstream, yanked off the fancy clothes, slipped out of the uncomfortable pumps, and eased into my comfy sweats. I caught sight of myself in the mirror and noticed that the pretty (well, sort of) made-up face had been replaced by pale, scared features.

By the time I'd put on a pot of coffee and settled onto my sofa, Wanda Sue had returned. Kong leaped onto my lap and buried his face under my arm, sighing in contentment. As I stroked his ears, the tension drained out of me like air from an overinflated balloon, and I related the evening's traumas to Wanda Sue.

As she listened, she brought a cup of steaming coffee over to me and seated herself next to me on the sofa. "Do you want to call Nick to tell him what happened with the coconut?"

My cheeks grew warm at the mention of his name, as I conjured up the passion that had flared between us outside the Taste of Venice. "I . . . I think I'll wait until morning. I need to get myself together first." In this state, I'd probably end up back in his arms again.

Wanda Sue's mouth turned up in a knowing smile. "I get you. He's just too hot to handle even when you're thinking straight." I tried not to smile myself as I got a load of her cold-weather outfit: skintight leggings and neon tunic, with a faux-fur jacket straining at the seams around her curves.

"Something like that." I looked down at Kong, not wanting Wanda Sue to read the truth of my feelings on my face. "I'll call him in the morning."

She sipped her coffee and unzipped the jacket. Her tunic had a huge black-and-white picture of Dolly Parton printed on the front. *Cute.*

"Sounds like a plan," Wanda Sue said. "Sometimes you have to remember that when life throws you a curve ball as crooked as a dog's leg, you just have to throw it back."

Huh?

My teacup poodle raised his head.

"She didn't mean you, Kong." At least, I didn't think so from what I could make out from that bizarre southernism. For a few quiet moments, I soothed him with some long strokes. "Okay, Wanda Sue, I've got two things to ask you. First, what's the story with the phantom Airstream next door? Is someone moving around from site to site?"

"Can't say." Her features took on a cagey expression. "You know I have to keep all my clients' identities private."

"Yeah, I remember when you had my parents living next door and never told me. That was a major freak-out."

"Sorry, hon."

"Okay, question two, and this one I really need to know the answer to, were you good friends with Beatrice's mother, Delores?"

"Oh, sure thing, I can tell you *that*." Her face brightened. "We were like two peas in a pod—bestest friends. She and I grew up here, and we got married about the same time, though she had a daughter and I didn't have any youngsters. But I was like a second mother to Beatrice."

"And she thinks the world of you," I assured her.

"I hope so," Wanda Sue said, and then she paused. "Anyway, as Delores and I grew older, we stayed friends. Even when she divorced that mean snake, Marco, we still met every week at Carlos' ice cream parlor. She'd order a big banana split, while I ate a measly little vanilla cone—and she never gained a pound. But I could have just applied the ice cream right here." She reached down and pinched her hips. "Just ain't right."

I wagged my head in agreement, anxious to hear the rest of the story. "And Delores died a few years ago, from lupus, right?"

"Yep. It was heart-wrenching." Wanda Sue's face crumpled into sad reflection. "She just withered away. Beatrice lost her mama, and I lost my best friend."

"I'm so sorry." And I meant it. Wanda Sue might dress like a tacky tropical version of her idol, Dolly Parton, but she had a heart of gold. "Was it awkward to meet in the ice cream store where Delores' ex-brother-in-law worked?"

Now it was Wanda Sue's turn to blush. "Not exactly."

"Okay, what's the story?" I made a "gimme" gesture with my hand.

"Delores and Carlos were . . . uh . . . more than friends—"

"Lovers?" I cut in excitedly. "They had a thing going?"

Wanda Sue exhaled in a long, drawn-out note of sorrow. "When they were teenagers, they fell in love. But Carlos got drafted and went to Vietnam as a helicopter pilot. He was a hunk."

"Carlos, a hunk?"

"He didn't weigh three hundred pounds then." She waved my question aside with some impatience. "Anyway, he was shot down, and they thought he was dead. So Marco moved in faster than fleas on a dog. He pushed Delores to get married, and I think she was still grieving too much to think straight."

I sat up, enthralled. "Go on. So when did Carlos come back?"

"A year after they were married." Wanda Sue folded her arms on her ample chest, her face kindling in anger. "Delores stuck with Marco 'cause of her religion, but she always loved Carlos. He was so kind. But Marco had a mean temper, and it just grew worse and worse over the years, and Delores . . . Well, she started up again with Carlos."

"So that's when they began the affair? How old were they?"

"Maybe in their thirties." She paused and shifted on the sofa as if the cushions had suddenly become made of cement.

"There's more?" I prompted.

"Beatrice is Carlos' daughter," she said in a flat voice. "That's why he loved her so much."

I sat back, stunned. *Desperate Housewives* had nothing on Coral Island.

"That's why the brothers had a falling-out. I think Marco knew. But I can't say for sure, 'cause Delores never told me."

"Did Delores and Carlos keep seeing each other?"

"Hon, they were star-cornered lovers. Nothing could've driven them apart." She smiled.

"Or star-crossed," I murmured.

"When Delores moved to town and finally decided to get a divorce, they spent all their time together—till she got sick. Even then, Carlos was at her side every step of the way, taking care of her right up to the moment she drew her last breath." Her smile faded. "My poor friend. She just never seemed to catch a break."

"But she did find true love," I pointed out in a soft voice.

"Yeah, I guess so."

We both fell silent for a few moments, with only the sound of Kong's doggy panting.

"Does Beatrice know?" I finally spoke up.

She sighed again. "Delores never told her."

I mulled over the revelations. Maybe Beatrice *had* found out and decided that Marco had to be eliminated— to avenge her mother's unhappiness *and* keep Guido with her. Could it be possible?

"Mallie, your face looks like you just sucked a lemon. What are you cooking up in your brain, girl?"

"Nothing." I gave myself a mental shake. Beatrice as a killer just didn't jibe with the girl I had met, unless she was an Oscar-winning actress of grief. "I suppose their story just seems so . . . sad."

"Like one of those Shakespeare-y tragedies."

Sort of.

I started to get us another cup of coffee, when a sudden pounding on my Airstream door startled me so much that I dropped my cup and it broke on the wood floor. Kong then awoke and began to bark.

"Who in the Sam Hill is that at this hour?" Wanda Sue exclaimed.

"Mallie, Mallie!" I heard a familiar voice yelling.

I cracked the door and saw Sandy, Jimmy, Madame Geri, and Anita—all shivering in the wind.

"Someone is trying to frame Jimmy," Sandy cried out. "He's going to be arrested!"

Chapter Nine

I swung the door open and hustled everyone inside my Airstream. One by one, they trooped in and found a spot on the sofa or nearby kitchen chair, all crammed tightly in the small confines of my trailer.

I scanned the clean-cut features of Jimmy, and next to him Sandy, worried and gnawing on a Snickers bar. Madame Geri appeared impassive, but I thought I detected a shadow of concern in her eyes. Hard to tell. Anita wasn't so difficult to read; she was filing her nails.

"What are you doing here?" I asked my boss.

"I was still in the office, ordering another jar of the bee cream, when Madame Geri came in—"

"If I were you, I'd lay off that stuff," I cut in. "Your face looks like a shriveled beet."

"Rosy glow," she responded, holding up her bony, wrinkled hands. "And it's smoothing out my cuticles too."

"Anita!" Sandy grabbed the nail file from her and threw it across the room. "This is my marriage and future husband's life at stake. Can you at least pretend to be interested?"

"Fine." She batted her almost nonexistent lashes. "I came along for the ride, but I guess I won't get a news story out of this debacle if I don't appear to give a rat's—"

"I could use some of that bee cream." Wanda Sue scanned Anita's red, swollen skin. "You don't seem to have so many deep lines under your eyes like you used to."

Anita glared at her. "You don't exactly have supermodel-smooth skin on your face, kid."

"Forget the bee cream—it's not good for you," Madame Geri said in a firm tone. "We're here for Jimmy."

"So what's going on?" I eased myself onto the floor, out of chairs and sofa space. "Who's framing Jimmy?"

"I don't know for sure," Madame Geri said. "After I took Pop Pop home, I had a partial message."

"Text? Telephone?" I inquired.

"Telepathy." She clamped her mouth in tight line. Anita rolled her eyes, and Wanda Sue crossed herself.

Silly me.

"Of course, I followed the spirit world's directions and went to the restaurant. But all they told me was that Jimmy was in danger of being blamed for Marco's death."

"You went back to the Taste of Venice?" My eyes widened. I couldn't imagine going back there for at least a year—enough time for the staff to forget what had happened. Well, maybe two years.

"No, Little Tuscany," she corrected me.

"I thought it was closed," Wanda Sue piped up.

"It is. Like that would stop me." A tiny smile lifted the corners of Madame Geri's mouth. "I went to Jimmy's locker and found this. . . ." We all leaned forward as she produced a clear plastic sandwich bag filled with some kind of garbage.

"Eww." Wanda Sue jerked back and held her nose. "Shrimp shells."

"That stinks to high heaven," Anita pointed out unnecessarily, as she whipped out a bee cream jar from her purse. "A little dab of this on my nose might take the smell away."

"You mean someone stashed those shells in Jimmy's locker so the police would think *he* placed the shrimp in Marco's sauce?" I spoke the words slowly, thinking aloud about the possible motivation. "It *was* a frame!"

"Exactly." Madame Geri raised her chin, her features kindled in anger.

"And you took the baggie out of Jimmy's locker?" Wanda Sue said with a touch of awe. "I would've been shaking in my shoes to do something like that. You're the bomb, Madame Geri."

Sandy and Jimmy nodded in agreement.

"Who had access to the restaurant?" I stretched my legs out in front of me, taking in a deep breath, as I tried to piece together a new set of suspects. "And Jimmy's locker?"

"Pretty much anybody, I'd think," said Madame Geri.

"The front door was unlocked." Madame Geri snatched the bee cream away from Anita. "If you put any more of this stuff near your nose, it'll fall off."

"Not likely." Anita produced another jar. "I keep two with me at all times—just in case I run out."

"Fine, I give up." Madame Geri tossed it at her, but Wanda Sue stretched out her hand and caught the jar.

"Oh, Anita, I forgot to tell you," Madame Geri added, "I had a message from your grandpa. He said to give Mallie a raise."

Anita gave a laugh of disbelief. "That skinflint? Not a chance in hell."

"That's not exactly where he is," Madame Geri added.

"Maybe I could try just a little bit of this bee cream?" Wanda Sue scanned the label for a few moments. "Doesn't say anything about side effects."

"You'll see. I tried to warn you." Madame Geri shrugged, then turned to me. "I locked up when I left the restaurant, but I couldn't say who might've been in there before me and got into Jimmy's locker."

"That doesn't help much." I watched Wanda Sue slather on a layer of the bee cream. "Except that we know the murderer is getting worried enough to implicate Jimmy."

"And try to kill Mallie," Wanda Sue added, her skin turning pink.

"What?!" everyone said at once.

"Didn't you see Rusty before you came in?" I scanned

the room. No one responded, and I gave an exclamation of impatience. "The whole windshield is cracked because someone threw a coconut at it while I was driving home from the Taste of Venice."

Sandy gasped.

"Did you see who it was?" Jimmy asked, patting Sandy's hand.

"Nope. They drove off too fast."

"And I'll bet it was the same person who tried to frame Jimmy," Madame Geri said.

"Another telepathic communiqué?" I couldn't help the sarcasm that crept into my tone.

She waved her hand in a dismissive gesture. "A lucky guess."

Wanda Sue began to scratch at her cheeks. "I feel all itchy."

"Your skin looks kind of blotchy," I pointed out, noticing the little red bumps that had just spread across her face. "It looks like . . . hives."

Instantly, she jumped up and dashed toward my bathroom; a small shriek followed as she strode back into the living room. "I've got measles!"

"No, it's that damn cream," I spat out. "You're having an allergic reaction." *Not another one!*

"Remember what happened to Mr. Santini," Jimmy added unnecessarily, his brow furrowing with concern.

"Mercy me." Wanda Sue clutched her face and moaned. "I'm too young to die."

"You're not that young," Anita said, tossing the bee

cream into her purse before I could snatch it away from her.

I rose to my feet. "We'd better get you to the ER, just to make sure you're okay."

Wanda Sue tapped her cheeks several times. "I've lost all feeling in my face—I can't wait. I'm calling 911." She flipped open her cell phone and punched in the numbers while we watched in helpless concern.

What next?

Two hours later, I drove Wanda Sue home from the ER. She'd been given Benadryl and a stern warning not to ever use bee cream again—or even look at a jar. (Okay, the latter was my suggestion.) By the time I made it back to my Airstream, it was after midnight, and all I wanted to do was curl up with Kong.

As I ducked inside my comfy home-on-wheels, I realized the air was almost as chilly as it was outdoors. Shivering, I toggled the thermostat a couple of times, but nothing happened.

Great. Just great.

The heater was on the fritz again.

After managing a few hours of sleep with the space heater chugging its meager puffs of warmth, I leaped out of bed at dawn and made a desperate call to Sam: "The heater is out again, and my Airstream is turning into an igloo. Help!" I crossed my fingers on both hands and looked up for divine support that the handyman might take pity on me.

I walked Kong, took a quick shower with the water as hot as I could possibly stand, dressed in the heaviest sweater and jeans that I could find, and hopped into my truck.

As the heat blasted out of Rusty's vents, I relaxed enough to focus on the roller coaster events of the night before.

Had I really been at a luxury dinner at the Taste of Venice, followed by a tiff that almost came to blows between the restaurant owner/possible murder suspect and the island psychic? Had I actually shared a passionate kiss with Nick Billie, followed by an attempt on my life by a coconut? Had I really ended up in the ER with my landlady, who had a reaction to bee cream?

Island life was anything but mellow.

As I breezed into the *Observer* office a few minutes later, Sandy was seated at her desk writing an obit, and I could hear Anita yakking on the phone from her office.

Business as usual.

Maybe I'd dreamed the whole series of events last night.

Sandy stopped typing and motioned me over to her desk. After looking around surreptitiously, she opened a desk drawer, and instead of seeing the usual stash of chocolate bars, I spied the plastic baggie with the shrimp shells.

So I didn't dream it after all.

"What are you doing keeping those things in the office?" I said, ramming the drawer shut.

She shrugged. "I didn't know what else to do with them. Madame Geri took Jimmy into town to talk with a lawyer, just in case he got called in by Nick Billie."

"Or she's questioned for tampering with evidence." I tossed my hobo bag onto my desk, causing the small stapler, notepad, and empty wallet to spill out. I tossed the stuff back in. "I'm impressed that Madame Geri even knows an attorney."

"He's a client. She's been communicating with his deceased brother for him."

"Of course." I seated myself and flipped on the computer.

"Hey, kiddo, you need to get that Taste of Venice review up on the blog ASAP." Anita stood at the doorway of her office, face red and peeling, matched now by a similar condition on her hands. I started to say something, then clamped my mouth shut again. What was the point?

I retrieved my notepad and held it up. "The details are all right here, at least as much as I could get before Madame Geri and Francesca started going at it."

"Sounds like the fight was the best part. Add that to the blog." She made a boxing jab at me, along with a little fancy footwork. "Keep it tight, none of that literature-major crap. And you can forget trying to have that crazy psychic get you a raise. If Grandpa were speaking from the dead, he'd be telling me to bump you down to minimum wage."

"Uh-huh."

"Was Wanda Sue okay?" Sandy asked, checking the desk drawer one more time, as if to make sure no one had taken the baggie in the last thirty seconds.

"She was fine, just a little embarrassed that she tried that stupid cream." I made sure my voice drifted in Anita's direction.

"It doesn't work for everybody," my editor commented before she disappeared into her office—no doubt to lay on another layer.

Sandy leaned forward and whispered, "She looks awful."

"It's a lost cause trying to tell her anything." I flipped open my notepad, noticing how my handwriting had grown almost illegible last night as the restaurant fight escalated. I squinted, trying to make out the last part.

"We're going to sit tight till the attorney tells Jimmy what to do," Sandy continued, leaning her elbows on a small stack of wedding magazines. "The wedding is still on. For now."

"It's going to happen, I just know it. And Jimmy is innocent, so you've got that on your side."

"Yeah." She was working hard to sound upbeat, but I knew Sandy too well. The little frown line between her eyebrows gave away her true emotional state, as did the tiny crumb of chocolate on her chin.

"Did you tell Nick about the coconut incident last night?"

I paused. "Not exactly."

"You'd better call him, just in case . . . uh, well, you

know . . . something else happens." She picked over her words as if she were tiptoeing over shells on a beach.

Torn between excitement and reluctance, I hesitated. After a few moments, though, both emotions took a backseat to the thought of another attempt on my life; it propelled me to pick up the receiver. As I punched in the police station's number, I tried to suppress the images that arose of my encounter last night with Nick outside the Taste of Venice. Heat crept into my face, and my heart began to thud like a bass drum.

Please don't let Nick answer. I wasn't ready to talk to him. Fortunately, I got his answering machine, and I blurted out, "Nick, someone tried to kill me last night by throwing a coconut through my windshield, but I'm fine now." I hung up.

"You might've given him a few more details," Sandy commented.

"I . . . I've got to get that Taste of Venice blog entry finished, or Anita will have my butt in a sling." That, at least, was true.

"Suit yourself, Mallie, but I think you're making a mistake." She opened one of the wedding magazines and began flipping through the pages. "Nick should know how desperate Marco's killer is getting."

"I'll go talk to him—if you come with me and spill the beans about the mystery shrimp shells in Jimmy's locker."

Sandy bit her lip and closed the magazine. "Point taken. Let's get back to work."

Satisfied, I resumed typing up my blog entry, and she resumed composing her obit. Nothing like a little reality check.

"Just be careful," Sandy warned, as her fingers flew across the keys. "I don't want you, or Jimmy, to be hurt."

"We'll be fine." I hoped my voice sounded more certain than I felt inside.

Sandy checked the drawer with the shrimp shells one more time. "Okay."

An hour later, I had the blog entry completed and sat back, scanning the lines for any errors or extraneous verbiage, knowing my nitpicking editor would check it over for any slight infraction of the Anita Grammar Police Rules. After three attempts at proofreading, I found only one spelling misdemeanor and a punctuation felony. I uploaded it with a triumphant click of the ENTER button.

The *Observer* Food Critic's Corner blog looked pretty good, if I had to say so myself. And I did.

Happily, I reread the reviews of Le Sink and Little Tuscany—*oops,* I spotted a typo in the Little Tuscany blog where I referenced Marco's secret sauce. It said *Marco's secret pauce. Yikes.* The only miracle was that Anita hadn't noticed it. As I made the correction, I noticed Beatrice had responded to the blog by pointing out that her Uncle Carlos had developed the sauce.

I blinked. Odd that no one had mentioned that to me. Odder still that Marco could actually make the sauce in his restaurant, unless Carlos had shared the recipe with him. And if Francesca had stolen the recipe for *her* sauce, how could she have taken it from Marco?

I jotted down those questions, puzzling over how the whole sauce thing might connect to Marco's death.

Tapping my pen on the desk, I pondered that one—to no avail. I left a message for Beatrice and pondered some more.

The office phone rang, startling me out of my reverie.

"Jimmy?" Sandy picked up, and I held my breath as she said "uh-huh" a few times. Then she hung up, her face glowing. "Madame Geri said it's going to be all right!"

I exhaled in relief. "Three cheers for the lawyer."

"No, it was the spirit world that finally told her things would be okay," she explained. "The lawyer said we had to provide the evidence for Nick—pronto. I'm going to meet them at the police station." She retrieved the plastic bag. "Are you coming with me?"

I checked my watch, stalling. Was I ready to see Nick? "It's almost noon. I need to walk Kong first."

Sandy stood up. "We'll wait for you."

"Great." Could I hook up my Airstream and head to South America in the next half hour?

Unlikely.

I closed out my computer, grabbed my hobo bag, and headed for the door, trying to hearten myself that at least I had finished a well-written, perfectly edited restaurant review for the blog.

"I found a typo in the Taste of Venice blog." Anita's words sang out from her office in glee.

I gritted my teeth.

Damn.

Half an hour later, still irritated that Anita had foiled me yet again, I drove up to my Airstream faster than I should have and jammed on the brakes.

My head jerked forward with Rusty's sudden halt.

Get a grip.

I slid out of my truck, hoping that Sam had dropped by to nurse my ailing heater back to health again. I saw a note on my Airstream, and a jolt of hope stirred inside my heart.

I snatched it off the door and read, *I need to see you. Cole.*

Oh.

"Hi," he said from behind me.

Turning slowly, I tried to prepare myself for that hurt look I had seen on his face last night. I wasn't wrong. His normally sunny, surfer-dude good looks appeared pinched and sad.

Guilt flooded through me. "I'd ask you in, but I don't think my heater is working."

"Sam was here about an hour ago, and I think he fixed it," he said, his voice flat.

"Well, let's get inside and warm up." I unlocked the door and scooped up Kong as we entered the Airstream.

Before I climbed the steps, I checked for that mystifying twin Airstream; it was parked there again! And I thought I spied a middle-aged woman inside, wearing an apron and holding up a retro-style Coke bottle. *Huh?*

"When did she check in?" I turned to Cole.

"Who?"

I pointed to the site next to me. Empty. What the hell was going on?

Hurrying inside, I motioned Cole to follow, and he shut the door behind us. Pushing all thoughts of the phantom Airstream out of my mind, I savored the warmth—and Kong's happy barks—for a brief few moments.

Once inside, I took a seat at the small kitchen table, and Cole sat across from me, still and silent.

I lifted Kong onto my lap. "I heard that you were going to do mug shots for Nick." I said. "That sounds really good, because you're such a wonderful photographer, and there's no one on the island who can do that. I'm sure it'll work out so you can make some extra cash and . . . uh . . ." My motormouth sputtered. The words sounded sort of phony, even to me.

"I haven't committed to the job yet. That was just his excuse for the dinner meeting, but he really wanted to know how things stood between us."

"Nick didn't tell me that."

"I let him know that we had unfinished business, but we weren't exactly committed—probably why he took the opportunity to steal a kiss at the restaurant."

I didn't answer, but I could feel the heat returning to my cheeks.

He took in a deep breath. "I've had a little time to sort out what's going on between us, and I want to ask you a question: Do you want me to stay?"

My mouth turned to cotton. I couldn't seem to form the words to respond.

"Look, I know I was the one who took off when we lived in Orlando, leaving you at Disney when you'd been demoted to a garbage sweeper—"

"I wasn't picking up garbage—only litter," I protested hotly.

"Whatever." He stretched his hands out to me. "We've always kept things light between us, but it doesn't mean what I feel for you is superficial. I love you, Mallie."

The words echoed around the Airstream like a ray of light bouncing from wall to wall.

Before I could stop myself, the corners of my lips turned up into a smile. Hey, it isn't every day that a girl is told she's loved. In fact, I'd heard it only once in my life, and that was when I was in college in St. Louis and one of the guys on the basketball team wanted to copy my American literature class notes.

Whoa. Now my internal motormouth had kicked in. That only happened during times of extreme emotion. Did that mean I really loved Cole, despite my attraction to Nick?

"Well?" he said, palms still open.

I placed my hands on top of his.

He toyed with my fingers. "Is that a yes? You want me to stay?"

"I . . . I don't know." My thoughts spun around as if in a tropical storm, swirling and confusing. Nothing seemed clear, least of all my feelings about Nick or Cole.

He squeezed my hands. "At least it's not a no, then?"

"Uh . . . uh . . ." My cell phone rang. It was Beatrice. "I need to get this call. Sorry."

"No problemo." He squared his shoulders, doing his best Terminator imitation.

I flipped open my phone. "Hi, Beatrice?"

"I got your message while Guido and I were at the funeral home. We're driving back to the house now." Her voice caught on a little sob, but she caught herself. "What's going on?"

Kong jumped off my lap, trotted over to Cole, and launched himself onto his lap. A sign? Shaking my head, I rose and walked into the kitchen area. "I was working on my blog for the Taste of Venice, and I noticed that you had added a comment to the Little Tuscany review."

"I . . . I had to tell the truth, even though I know Dad wouldn't have liked it." Her words came out haltingly. "I noticed that you said my father developed the secret sauce recipe. It was Uncle Carlos who came up with the ingredients."

"For real?" My hands tightened around the cell phone

in excitement. "Did he share the recipe with Francesca?"

"I don't think so, but she did win all that money for *her* sauce, which seemed similar. . . ." Beatrice hesitated. "Maybe she stole the recipe from Uncle Carlos, but he never said anything."

"What about your dad? Did he have the actual ingredient list?"

"No. I'd have to swing by Uncle Carlos' house on the day before we needed the sauce. He made it from scratch at his house, and then I'd take it to the restaurant, put it in the fridge, the flavors would settle overnight, and Dad would add a few herbs of his own the next day, taste it, and then serve it." She gave a small laugh. "Just so it had *his* stamp."

"So the day your uncle died of the heart attack, you picked up the sauce at his house?" My breathing spiked into a tumult. "Was there anything odd that you noticed that morning?"

She didn't respond. "Not really. He said he'd had some visitors that morning."

"Who?" I almost shouted.

"He didn't say. Guido was with me; let me ask him." She must have covered the phone, because I could hear Guido's muffled words in the background. "He didn't tell Guido anything either."

"Do you think it could've been Francesca? She might have been there, trying to cover up that she stole the recipe—and then doctored the sauce to knock off Marco, so he couldn't rat her out," I said in a rush of words. "That's why she got so incensed with Madame Geri last night."

"M-maybe."

"Could you give me your uncle's address and meet me there?"

"Sure. It's at Gumbo Limbo Preserve, one of those senior neighborhoods not far from the Twin Palms." Oh, yeah, I'd passed it many times: a "manufactured"-home—translated: trailer—community for those fifty-five and older. Lots of bingo, shuffleboard, and water aerobics. And an ambulance stationed at the gatehouse.

Beatrice gave me the street and house number. "Guido and I can get there in about thirty minutes; we'll let the security guy know you're coming."

"Great." I hung up, grinning wildly at Cole. "It was Francesca all along! She killed Marco after Carlos died, so she'd be the only one with the secret sauce recipe."

Cole cast a doubtful glance at me. "You think she would have killed someone over a sauce?"

"It was worth fifty thousand dollars, maybe more. Enough for her to try to frame Jimmy and attempt to kill me," I added, filling him in on the shrimp shells and the coconut incident, while I reached for my purse and truck keys. "I'm heading over to Carlos'."

He stood up and placed Kong on the floor. "I'm going with you. This could be dangerous."

"We'll call Nick on the way," I said, causing an

immediate wince by Cole, as if I'd sucker punched him. "For police protection only."

Cole's mouth fastened into a thin line. "Sure."

I couldn't focus on him right now. I had a murderer to catch.

And time was running out.

Chapter Ten

Cole and I hopped into Rusty and drove toward Carlos' house, not saying a word. I did notice that he traced the cracked windshield with his forefinger but didn't comment. The cracks had deepened, but I still had enough room to see the road.

About halfway there, I flipped open my cell phone and called Nick to let him know we were heading to Marco's house. He didn't answer, so I left him a voice mail.

We arrived at the entrance, waving at the skinny, white-haired security guy wearing a name tag that read RORY. We gave him our names, and he lifted the gate.

"You know, this windshield looks like it's taken some damage." Rory slipped on a pair of reading glasses to get a better look and tapped on the windshield. "Yep, it's damaged, all right." The cracks expanded.

"Thanks. I noticed." Accelerating slowly, I pulled away.

"You have to wonder what he sees without the glasses," Cole commented.

I laughed, finding the street easily. But the house was another matter. Each "manufactured" home was spaced about six inches apart, identical in appearance, with all the mailboxes on one side of the road. So it was nearly impossible to tell which box went with what house. Almost pounding the wheel in frustration, I reached for the cell phone to call Beatrice again, when an aging couple passed me on a tandem bike, wearing identical powder-blue warm-up suits.

I stopped and rolled down the window. "Hi, could you tell me where Carlos Santini lived?"

"Last house on the left," the woman answered as she extended a pointed finger in the direction of a black Buick Regal. "That woman just asked us the same question."

My glance darted up the street, just in time to see Francesca disappear through the front door of Carlos' house.

Busted!

"Cole, call Nick again." I handed my cell phone to him. "I think we've caught Francesca red-handed."

"Okay, but let's wait until he gets here to do anything," Cole urged as he hit the REDIAL button. "We don't know what's going on."

Ignoring his warning, I coasted toward Carlos' house. Using the gas pedal would be a dead giveaway with Rusty's aging, chugging engine.

I stopped about two houses down from where Francesca had parked her car, which meant about fifty feet separated our vehicles. Turning off the engine, I peered through the hazy, semi-shattered windshield to monitor Francesca's whereabouts.

"Damn, I can't make out much of anything." I poked my head out the window. It still didn't help.

"Just sit tight," Cole said. "I left Nick a message, telling him to get here right away."

Drumming my fingers against the steering wheel, I felt the minutes tick by. No Beatrice. No Guido. No Nick. If I waited much longer, Francesca might be able to cover her tracks and whatever she had done to steal Carlos' secret sauce.

"I can't wait!" I exclaimed, jerking open my door.

"Mallie—stop!"

But I was already making a beeline for Carlos' place, jogging across the tiny front yards of his neighbors. When I reached my destination, I crept toward the front of the house, squinting to see through the jalousie window. I couldn't see anything, but I heard Francesca moving around through the thin walls.

Tiptoeing around the side of the house, I tried another window. *Eureka!* Francesca stood there, leaning over a desk in the living room, as she tossed and sifted through a stack of papers.

I'd wager my nonexistent raise that she was looking for the recipe.

I glanced back at my truck; Cole had jumped out and was heading in my direction, shouting on his cell phone.

Oh no!

Francesca would hear him, and she might try to escape. Waving both arms, I motioned him to stay back. But he kept coming.

Taking in a deep breath, I circled back to the front door and burst into the house.

"Caught you!" I yelled out. Shaken, Francesca slapped a hand against her chest, causing her to drop a small 3×5 card.

"You nearly gave me a heart attack, you nutcase," she snarled.

"Serves you right." I bent down to retrieve the card, but she reached for it at the same time. We knocked heads and staggered back.

Dazed, I rubbed my scalp. She did likewise but took an extra couple of seconds to clear her head—just long enough for me to pick up the card.

"Give me that! *Now!*" Her face crinkled with a vicious expression. "It's mine."

Backing up a few steps, I glanced down at the old-fashioned handwriting on the card. *Yes!* "It's Carlos' recipe for his secret sauce. I knew it! You're were trying to hide the evidence, because you stole it from him, and then you murdered Marco to silence him forever."

"You're crazy."

"You're a thief and a killer!" I held out the recipe card like a talisman. "And here's the proof."

"Carlos *gave* me that recipe, you idiot, so I could win

the cooking contest, win the fifty thousand dollars, and open my restaurant."

I laughed as I placed my hands on my hips. "And why would he do that?"

"Because he hated Marco and wanted my restaurant to compete with his."

"Then why did you come here to steal the recipe card?" I waved it in her face.

Her dark eyes narrowed. "It's the only copy, and I didn't want anyone else to have it. Even Beatrice doesn't know what's in that sauce. I could market it all over the world as Francesca's Five-Herb Sauce and make millions."

"So you're a killer *and* a swindler!" I exclaimed.

She screamed something in Italian and lunged at me, trying to seize the recipe. I whipped it behind my back, holding out the other arm to fend her off. She slapped my hand away, spitting Italian obscenities (not hard for me to translate), as she picked up a large antique book that had been lying on the desk.

Francesca swung it at me, but I ducked, calling out for Cole. Then she grasped the book in both hands and came at me, holding it out like a battering ram. I sidestepped her attack, but she couldn't halt the momentum— and ended up slamming against a wall. Amazingly, she didn't drop the book.

"Mallie!" Cole and Nick said in unison as they appeared at the front door.

Francesca took the opportunity to hurl the book at my head. I hit the floor, but the book kept going and flew toward Cole and Nick. They jumped to either side, and the book winged its way through the door, where it came to rest on the lawn.

"You!" Nick pointed at Francesca. "Get on the floor, and put your hands behind your back."

She immediately dropped down, whimpering.

"Cuff her!" I shouted. "She killed Marco and came here to steal the secret sauce recipe! And I'll bet she's the one who tried to frame Jimmy and threw that coconut at my truck."

"Not true," she responded, face muffled by the carpet. She turned her head. "At least the killing part. I did put the shrimp shells in Jimmy's locker, and I threw the coconut at your rusty old truck to scare you enough to back off. You were getting too close to the truth behind the secret sauce. But I didn't murder Marco."

"Liar!" I retorted.

Cole retrieved the book and strolled back inside. "This is one lethal tome."

I took it from him and curled my hands around the hand-tooled leather cover, keeping it safely away from my assailant.

Nick handcuffed Francesca and hauled her to her feet.

"I only wanted the damn recipe, so I could win 'Taste of the Island' Best Sauce, market it, and become a millionaire with my own TV show," she muttered, glowering at me.

"Says you." I clutched the book even tighter, glancing down at the title. Dante's *Inferno*. Fitting. "This is evidence."

"I'll take that," Nick said in a calm voice. As I handed it to him, a letter slipped out and floated toward the floor, as gracefully as a palm frond dropping to the earth.

Puzzled, I caught the folded letter before it landed on the carpet.

"Mallie, don't—" Nick began, but I was already reading it aloud.

"My Dear Beatrice,

When you read this letter, I will be gone. The doctor told me it was a matter of days. But do not grieve, my dear. I'm ready to join your mother, my beloved Delores. She was my soul mate, and you are the child of our love. And that is why I could not allow Marco to divide you and Guido. I put the shrimp in my secret sauce, knowing he would taste it and die. I know I will pay for this sin, but I hope you will forgive me.

Dio volente.
All my love,
Your father."

My mouth dropped open, and I glanced up to behold Beatrice and Guido standing there, realization dawning in their eyes.

She gasped, and Guido made a choking sound. I managed to sputter an apology as I handed Beatrice the letter.

"I told you I didn't kill Marco," Francesca grated out between clenched teeth. "All I did was try to steal the recipe card."

"And commit attempted battery—with a coconut and a book," Nick added in a grim tone.

"Did you know that Carlos killed his brother?" I demanded of Nick, anger welling up inside of me.

"Only this afternoon, when I received Carlos' confession in the mail. He must have sent it the day he died. He also stated that he left the letter for Beatrice in the Dante book on his desk. That's why I tried to stop you." Nick lifted one dark eyebrow. "If you had just waited and talked to me before coming over here half-cocked, I could have told you."

"Like when? How can I trust that you would have let me in on it?"

"That's the problem, isn't it—trust?" Nick said, regarding me with a hushed silence before steering Francesca out of the house.

Beatrice took Guido's hand and solemnly placed the letter in his palm. Then they slowly exited the house as well.

Cole put his arms around me, and I buried my face in his chest. "I messed up big-time again, didn't I?" I moaned.

"Not really. Your heart's in the right place." He smoothed my curls with a loving, soft caress. "With me."

I pulled back in disbelief. "After all of this, you still care?"

"You bet. We belong together."

Maybe he was right.

Epilogue

The cold snap finally ended, just in time for the "Taste of the Island," as well as Jimmy and Sandy's soon-to-be wedding.

As I sat outside my Airstream in my yellow sundress, waiting for Cole, I tilted my head back to enjoy the afternoon heat. It was amazing how quickly the Florida sun could brush away any lingering chill with its sultry, sweeping warmth.

The sunshine reflected off Rusty's spanking-new windshield, and I savored the sight of my truck's restored condition. It almost banished the bad memories of the coconut attack last week.

Unfortunately, it would take longer for me to forget how stupidly I had bungled the events at Carlos' house.

Dumb. Dumb. Dumb.

Just then, Wanda Sue strolled up with Madame Geri. "Are you ready to head out to the 'Taste of the Island'?"

"As soon as Cole gets here." I sighed. "What a week. Can you believe what happened?"

"Yeah, who would have thunk it?" Wanda Sue sat next to me, fanning herself with a large straw sun hat.

"I didn't get the whole story from the spirit world," said Madame Geri. "Not about Carlos and Marco, and not about your raise," she said, turning to me. "Turns out Anita's grandfather *was* a skinflint."

"Not surprising." I slathered sunblock on my face to avoid more freckles and handed the bottle to Wanda Sue.

"I still can't find it in myself to blame Carlos. He did it for Beatrice, so she could have the life he never had with Delores. It's kind of touching in a way." Wanda Sue sighed as she squirted a huge blob of sunblock into her palm. "I've got to be careful with the sun since that bee cream disaster."

I nodded. "You don't want to end up with another allergic reaction."

Wanda Sue visibly shuddered.

"I told you, the Coral Island bees don't create honey that agrees with humans," Madame Geri stated, her mouth pursed.

"Except for Anita's skin." I hated to say it, but two days ago, her face finally stopped peeling, and she looked ten years younger. Wouldn't you just know?

"Guess I was wrong about that one too," Madame Geri admitted.

I checked my watch, wondering where Cole was. Then I took a peep at the site next door. The phantom Airstream was back! And so was the middle-aged woman in the apron.

"Look, she's right there!" I pointed at my neighbor. Wanda Sue didn't glance up.

But Madame Geri waved at her. "It's Maude Butterman. She used to keep her Airstream here at the Twin Palms."

I flashed an accusatory glance at my landlady. "I thought you told me no one had checked in."

"She didn't," Wanda Sue said, meeting my eyes with a sheepish expression. "Remember our conversation about Maude Butterman?"

"Maybe." I took another look at the Airstream. It had vanished. "Okay, what's going on?"

"Maude didn't 'check in.' She died about ten years ago," Madame Geri explained. "She and her husband honeymooned here in the fifties, but they liked it so much, they stayed. She reappears whenever there's going to be a wedding on the island."

"Oh." What else could I say?

Wanda Sue spread her hands in helpless appeal. "Sorry, Mallie. I didn't think you'd believe me if I told you the rest of the story about Mrs. Butterman. I guess she's here because of Sandy and Jimmy."

"Hi." Cole cruised onto my site, wearing a tropical shirt and knee-length surfer shorts. He grinned at me, holding out a small box. "Mallie, will you marry me?"

Omigod.